HER
ROYAL WEDDING
WISH

HER
ROYAL WEDDING
WISH

BY

CARA COLTER

MILLS & BOON®

Pure reading pleasure™

First published in Great Britain 2008
Large Print edition 2008
Harlequin Mills & Boon Limited,
Eton House, 18-24 Paradise Road,
Richmond, Surrey TW9 1SR

© Cara Colter 2008

ISBN: 978 0 263 20089 8

Set in Times Roman 16½ on 20 pt.
16-1008-47477

Printed and bound in Great Britain
by Antony Rowe Ltd, Chippenham, Wiltshire

In memory of Hunter
1997–2007
Beloved.

CHAPTER ONE

JAKE Ronan took a deep, steadying breath, the same kind he would take and hold right before *the* shot or *the* assault or *the* jump.

No relief. His heart was beating like a deer three steps ahead of a wolf pack. His palms were slick with sweat.

He was a man notorious for keeping his cool. And in the past three years that notoriety had served him well. He'd taken a hijacked plane back from the bad guys, jumped from ten thousand feet in the dead of night into territory controlled by hostiles, rescued fourteen school-children from a hostage taking.

But in the danger-zone department nothing did

him in like a wedding. He shrugged, rolled his shoulders, took another deep breath.

His old friend, Colonel Gray Peterson, recently retired, the reason Ronan was here on the tiny tropical-island paradise of B'Ranasha, shifted uneasily beside him. Under his breath he said a word that probably had never been said in a church before. "You don't have your *sideways* feeling, do you?" Gray asked.

Ronan was famous among this tough group of men, his comrades-in-arms, for the *feeling,* a sixth sense that warned him things were about to go wrong, in a big way.

"I just don't like weddings," he said, keeping his voice deliberately hushed. "They make me feel uptight."

Gray contemplated that as an oddity. "Jake," he finally said reassuringly, his use of Ronan's first name an oddity in itself, "it's not as if you're the one getting married. You're part of the security team. You don't even know these people."

Ronan had never been the one getting married, but his childhood had been littered with his mother's latest attempt to land the perfect man. His own longing for a normal family, hidden under layers of adolescent belligerence, had usually ended in disillusionment long before the day of yet another elaborate wedding ceremony, his mother exchanging starry-eyed "I do's" with yet another temporary stepfather.

Ronan had found a family he enjoyed very much when he'd followed in his deceased father's footsteps, over his mother's strenuous and tear-filled protests, and joined the Australian military right out of high school. Finally, there had been structure, predictability and genuine camaraderie in his life.

And then he'd been recruited for a multinational military unit that was a first-response team to world crises. The unit, headquartered in England, was comprised of men from the most elite special forces units around the world. They had members from the British Forces SAS, from the French Foreign Legion, from the U.S. SEALs and Delta Force.

His family became a tight-knit brotherhood of warriors. They went where angels feared to go; they did the work no one else wanted to do; they operated in the most dangerous and troubled places in the world. As well as protecting world figures at summits, conferences, peace talks, they dismantled bombs, gathered intelligence, took back planes, rescued hostages, blew up enemy weapons caches. They did the world's most difficult work. They did it quickly, quietly and anonymously. There were few medals, little acknowledgment, no back-patting ceremonies.

But there was: brutal training, exhausting hours, months of deep cover and more danger than playing patty-cake with a rattlesnake.

When Ronan had been recruited, he had said a resounding yes. A man knew exactly when his natural-born talents intersected with opportunity, and from his first day in the unit, code-named Excalibur, he had known he had found what he was born to do.

A family, other than his brothers in arms, was out of the question. This kind of work was unfair to the women who were left at home. A man so committed to a dangerous lifestyle was not ready to make the responsibilities of a family and a wife his priority.

Which was a happy coincidence for a man who had the wedding *thing* anyway. Ronan's most closely guarded secret was that he, fearless fighting man, pride of Excalibur, would probably faint from pure fright if he ever had to stand at an altar like the one at the front of this church as a groom. As a man waiting for his bride.

So far, no one was standing at it, though on this small island, traditions were slightly reversed. He'd been briefed to understand that the bride would come in first and wait for the groom.

Music, lilting and lovely, heralded her arrival, but above the notes Ronan heard the rustle of fabric and slid a look down the aisle of the church. A vision in ivory silk floated slowly toward them. The dress, the typical wedding costume of the Isle of B'Ranasha, covered the bride from head to toe. It was unfathomable how something so unrevealing could be so sensual.

But it was. The gown clung to the bride's slight curves, accentuated the smooth sensuality of her movements. It was embroidered in gold thread that caught the light and thousands of little pearls that shimmered iridescently.

The reason Ronan was stationed so close to the altar was that this beautiful bride, Princess Shoshauna of B'Ranasha, might be in danger.

Since retiring from Excalibur, Gray had taken the position as head of security for the royal family of B'Ranasha. With the upcoming wedding, he'd asked Ronan if he wanted to take some leave and help provide extra security. At first Gray had presented the job as a bit of a lark—beautiful island, beautiful women, unbeatable climate, easy job, lots of off-time.

But by the time Ronan had gotten off the plane, the security team had intercepted a number of threats aimed directly at the princess, and Gray had been grim-faced and tense. The colonel was certain they were generating from within the palace itself, and that a serious security breach had developed within his own team.

"Look at the lady touching the flowers," Gray said tersely.

Ronan spun around, amazed by how much discipline it took to take his eyes off the shimmering vision of that bride. A woman at the side of the church was fiddling with a bouquet of flowers. She kept glancing nervously over her shoulder, radiating tension.

There it was, without warning, that sudden downward dip in his stomach, comparable to a ten-story drop on a roller coaster.

Sideways.

Surreptitiously Ronan checked his weapon, a 9mm Glock, shoulder holstered. Gray noticed, cursed under his breath, tapped his own hidden weapon, a monstrosity that members of Excalibur liked to call the Cannon.

Ronan felt himself shift, from a guy who hated weddings to one hundred percent warrior. It was moments exactly like this that he trained for.

The bride's gown whispered as she walked to the front.

Gray gave him a nudge with his shoulder. "You're on her," he said. "I'm on the flower lady."

Ronan nodded, moved as close to the altar as he could without drawing too much attention to himself. Now he could smell the bride's perfume, tantalizing, as exotic and beautiful as the abundant flowers that bloomed in profusion in every open space of this incredible tropical hideaway.

The music stopped. Out of the corner of his eye, he saw the flower lady duck. *Now,* he thought, and felt every muscle tense and coil, *ready.*

Nothing happened.

An old priest came out of the shadows at the front of the chapel, his golden face tranquil, his eyes crinkled with good humor and acceptance.

He wore the red silk robe of a traditional B'Ranasha monk.

Ronan felt Gray's tension beside him. They exchanged glances. Gray's hand now rested inside his jacket. His facade of complete calm did not fool Ronan. His buddy's hand was now resting on the Cannon. Despite the unchanging expression on Gray's face, Ronan felt the shift in mood, recognized it as that *itching* for action, battle fever.

The sideways feeling in Ronan's stomach intensified. His brain did a cool divide, right down the middle. One part of him watched the priest, the bride. The groom would arrive next. One part of him smelled perfume and noted the exquisite detail on her silk dress.

On the other side of the divide, Ronan had become pure predator, alert, edgy, ready.

The bride lifted her veil, and for just a split second his warrior edge was gone. Nothing could have prepared Jake Ronan for the fact he was looking into the delicate, exquisite perfect features of Princess Shoshauna of B'Ranasha.

His preparation for providing security for the wedding had included learning to recognize all the members of the royal families, especially the prospective bride and groom, but there had never been any reason to meet them.

He had been able to view Shoshauna's photographs with detachment: young, pretty, pampered. But those photos had not prepared him for her in the flesh. Her face, framed by a shimmering black waterfall of straight hair, was faintly golden and flawless. Her eyes were almond shaped, tilted upward, and a shade of turquoise he had seen only once before, in a bay where he'd surfed in his younger days off the coast of Australia.

She blinked at him, then looked to the back of the room.

He yanked himself away from the tempting vision of her. It was very bad to lose his edge, his sense of mission, even for a split second. A warning was sounding deep in his brain.

And in answer to it, the back door of the

church whispered open. Ronan glanced back. Not the prince. A man in black. A hood over his face. A gun.

Long hours of training had made Ronan an extremely adaptable animal. His mission instantly crystallized; his instincts took over.

His mission became to protect the princess. In an instant she was the focus of his entire existence. If he had to, he would lay down his life to keep her safe. No hesitation. No doubt. No debate.

The immediate and urgent goal: remove Princess Shoshauna from harm's way. That meant for the next few minutes, things were going to get plenty physical. He launched himself at her, registered the brief widening of those eyes, before he shoved her down on the floor, shielding her body with his own.

Even beneath the pump of pure adrenaline, a part of him *felt* the exquisite sweetness of her curves, felt a need beyond the warrior's response trained into him—something far more primal and male— to protect her fragility with his own strength.

A shot was fired. The chapel erupted into bedlam.

"Ronan, you're covered," Gray shouted. "Get her out of here."

Ronan yanked the princess to her feet, put his body between her and the attacker, kept his hand forcefully on the fragile column of her neck to keep her down.

He got himself and the princess safely behind the relative protection of the stone altar, pushed her through an opening into the priest's vestibule. There Ronan shattered the only window and shoved Princess Shoshauna through it, trying to protect her from the worst of the broken glass with his own arm.

Her skirt got caught, and most of it tore away, which was good. Without the layers of fabric, he discovered she could run like a deer. They were in an alleyway. He kept his hand at the small of her back as they sprinted away from the church. In the background he heard the sound of three more shots, screams.

The alley opened onto a bright square, postcard pretty, with white stucco storefronts, lush palms, pink flowers the size of basketballs. A cabdriver, oblivious to the backdrop of firecracker noises, was in his front seat, door open, slumbering in the sun. Ronan scanned the street. The only other vehicle was a donkey cart for tourists, the donkey looking as sleepy as the cabdriver.

Ronan made his decision, pulled the unsuspecting driver from his cab and shoved the princess in. She momentarily got hung up on the gearshift. He shoved her again, and she plopped into the passenger seat. He then jumped in behind her, turned the key and slammed the vehicle into gear.

Within seconds the sounds of gunfire and the shouted protests of the cabdriver had faded in the distance, but he kept driving, his brain pulling up maps of this island as if he had an Internet search program.

"Do you think everyone's all right back there?" she asked. "I'm worried about my grandfather."

Her English was impeccable, her voice a silk

scarf—soft, sensual, floating across his neck as if she had actually touched him.

He shrugged the invisible hand away, filed it under *interesting* that she was more worried about her grandfather than the groom. And he red-flagged it that the genuine worry on her face made him feel a certain unwanted softness for her.

Softness was not part of his job, and he liked to think not part of his nature, either, trained out of him, so that he could make clinical, precise decisions that were not emotionally driven. On the other hand he'd been around enough so-called important people to be able to appreciate her concern for someone other than herself.

"No one was hit," he said gruffly.

"How could you know that? I could hear gunfire after we left."

"A bullet makes a different sound when it hits than when it misses."

She looked incredulous and skeptical. "And with everything going on, you were listening for that?"

"Yes, ma'am." Not listening for that *exactly,*

but listening. He had not heard the distinctive *ka-thunk* of a hit, nor had he heard sounds that indicated someone badly hurt. Details. Every member of Excalibur was trained to pay attention to details that other people missed. It was amazing how often something that seemed insignificant could mean the difference between life and death.

"My grandfather has a heart problem," she said softly, worried.

"Sorry." He knew he sounded insincere, and at this moment he was. He only cared if one person was safe, and that was her. He was not risking a distraction, a misdirection of energy, by focusing on anything else.

As if to challenge his focus, his cell phone vibrated in his pocket. He had turned it off for the wedding, because his mother had taken to leaving him increasingly frantic messages that she had *big* news to share with him. Big news in her life always meant one thing: a new man, the proclamation it was *different* this time, more extravagant wedding plans.

Some goof at Excalibur, probably thinking it was funny, had given her his cell number against his specific instructions. But a glance at the caller ID showed it was not his mother but Gray.

"Yeah," he answered.

"Clear here."

"Here, too. Aurora—" he named the princess in Sleeping Beauty, a reference that was largely cultural, that might not be understood by anyone listening "—is fine."

"Excellent. We have the perp. No one injured. The guy was firing blanks. He could have been killed. What kind of nutcase does that?"

He contemplated that for a moment and came up with *one who wants to stop the wedding.* "Want me to bring her back in? Maybe they could still go ahead with the ceremony."

Details. The princess flinched ever so slightly beside him.

"No. Absolutely not. Something's wrong here. Really wrong. Nobody should have been able to penetrate the security around that wedding. It has to be someone within the palace, so I don't want her back here until I know who it is. Can you keep her safe until I get to the bottom of it?"

Ronan contemplated that. He had a handgun and two clips of ammunition. He was a stranger to the island and was now in possession of a stolen vehicle, not to mention a princess.

Despite circumstances not being anywhere near perfect, he knew in his business perfect circumstances were in short supply. It was a game of odds, and of trust in one's own abilities. "Affirmative," he said.

"I can't trust my phone, but we can probably use yours once more to give you a time frame and set a rendezvous."

"All right." He should have hung up, but he made the mistake of glancing at her pinched face. "Ah, Gray? Is her grandfather all right?"

"Slamming back the Scotch." Gray lowered his voice, "Though he actually seems a little, er, pleased, that his granddaughter didn't manage to get married."

Ronan pocketed his phone. "Your grandfather's fine."

"Oh, that's wonderful news! Thank you!"

"I can't take you back just yet, though."

Some finely held tension disappeared from her shoulders, as if she allowed herself to start breathing after holding her breath.

Eyes that had been clouded with worry, suddenly tilted upward when she smiled. If he was not mistaken, and he rarely was, given his gift with details, a certain mischief danced in their turquoise depths.

She did not inquire about the groom, and now that her concerns for her grandfather had been relieved, she didn't look anything like a woman who had just had her wedding ceremony shattered by gunfire, her dress shredded. In fact, she looked downright happy. As if to confirm that conclusion, she took off her bridal headdress, held it out the window and let the wind take it. She laughed with delight as it floated behind them, children chasing it down the street.

The wind billowing through the open window caught at the tendrils of her hair, and she shook it all free from the remaining pins that held it, and it spilled down over the slenderness of her shoulders.

If he was not mistaken, Princess Shoshauna was very much enjoying herself.

"Look, Your Highness," he said, irritated. "This is not a game. Don't be throwing anything else out the window that will make us easy to follow or remember."

She tossed her hair and gave him a look that was faintly mutinous. Obviously, because of her position, she was not accustomed to being snapped at. But that was too bad. There was only room for one boss here, and it wasn't going to be her.

With the imminent danger now at bay, at least temporarily, his thought processes slowed, and he began to sort information. His assessment of the situation wasn't good. He had been prepared to do a little wedding security, not to find himself in possession of a princess who had someone trying to kill her.

He didn't know the island. He had no idea where he could take her where it would be secure. He had very little currency, and at some point he was going to have to feed her, and get her out of that all-too-attention-grabbing outfit. He had to assume that whoever was after her would be sophisticated enough to trace credit card use. Ditto for his cell phone. They could use it once more to arrange a time and place for a rendezvous and then he'd have to pitch it. On top of that, he had to assume this vehicle had already been reported stolen; it would have to be ditched soon.

On the plus side, she was alive, and he planned to keep it that way. He had a weapon, but very little ammunition.

He was going to have to use the credit card once. To get them outfitted. By the time it was traced, they could be a long way away.

"Do you have any enemies?" he asked her. If he had one more phone call with Gray, maybe he could have some information for him. Plus, it would help him to know if this threat was about something personal or if it was politically motivated. Each of those scenarios made for a completely different enemy.

"No," she said, but he saw the moment's hesitation.

"No one hates you?"

"Of course not." But again he sensed hesitation, and he pushed.

"Who do you think did this?" he asked. "What's your gut feeling?"

"What's a gut feeling?" she asked, wide-eyed.

"Your instinct."

"It's silly."

"Tell me," he ordered.

"Prince Mahail was seeing a woman before he asked me to marry him. She's actually a cousin of mine. She acted happy for me, but—"

Details. People chose to ignore them, which was too bad. "Your instincts aren't silly," he told her gruffly. "They could keep you alive. What's her name?"

"I don't want her to get in trouble. She probably has nothing to do with this."

The princess wasn't just choosing to ignore her instincts, but seemed *determined* to. Still, he appreciated her loyalty.

"She won't be in trouble." *If she didn't do anything.* "Her name?"

"Mirassa," she said, but reluctantly.

"Now tell me how to find a market. A small one, where I can get food. And something for you to wear."

"Oh," she breathed. "Can I have shorts?" She blinked at him, her lashes thick as a chimney brush over those amazing ocean-bay eyes.

He tried not to sigh audibly. Wasn't that just like a woman? Even a crisis could be turned into an opportunity to shop!

"I'm getting what draws the least attention to you," he said, glancing over at her long legs exposed by her torn dress. "I somehow doubt that's going to be shorts."

"Am I going to wear a disguise?" she asked, thrilled.

She was determined not to get how serious this was. And maybe that was good. The last thing he needed was hysteria.

"Sure," he said, going along, "you get to wear a disguise."

"You could pretend to be my boyfriend," Princess Shoshauna said, with way too much enthusiasm. "We could rent a motorcycle and blend in with the tourists. How long do you think you'll have to hide me?"

"I don't know yet. Probably a couple of days."

"Oh!" she said, pleased, determined to perceive this life-and-death situation as a grand adventure. "I have always wanted to ride a motorcycle!"

The urge to strangle her was not at all in keeping with the businesslike, absolutely emotionless attitude he needed to have around her. That attitude would surely be jeopardized further by pretending to be her boyfriend, by sharing a motorcycle with her. His mind went there—her pressed close, her crotch pressed into the small of his back, the bike throbbing underneath them.

Buck up, soldier, he ordered himself. *There's going to be no motorcycle.*

"I'll cut my hair," she decided.

It was the first reasonable idea she had presented, but he was aware he wasn't even considering it. Her hair was long and straight, jet-black and glossy. Her hair was glorious. He wasn't letting her cut her hair, even if it would be the world's greatest disguise.

He knew he was making that decision for all the wrong reasons, and that his professionalism had just slipped the tiniest little notch. There was no denying the *sideways* feeling seemed to have taken up permanent residence in his stomach.

Shoshauna slid the man who was beside her a look and felt the sweetest little dip in the region of her stomach. He was incredibly good-looking. His short hair was auburn, burnt brown with strands of red glinting as the sun struck it. His eyes, focused on the road, were topaz colored, like a lion's. As if the eyes were not hint enough of his strength, there was the formidable set of his lips, the stubborn set of his chin, the flare of his nostrils.

He was a big man, broad and muscled, not like the slighter men of B'Ranasha. When he had thrown her onto the floor of the chapel, she had felt the shock first. No man had ever touched her like that before! Technically, it had been more a tackle than a touch. But then she had become aware of the hard, unforgiving lines of him, felt the strange and forbidden thrill of his male body shielding hers.

Even now she watched as his hands found their way to his necktie, tugged impatiently at it. He loosened it, tugged it free, shoved it in his pocket. Next, he undid the top button of his shirt, rubbed his neck as if he'd escaped the hangman's noose.

"What's your name?" she asked. It was truly shocking, considering how aware she'd felt of him, within seconds of marrying someone else.

She glanced at his fingers, was entranced by the shape of them, the faint dusting of hair on the knuckles. Shocked at herself, she realized she could imagine them tangling in her hair.

Of course, she had led a somewhat sheltered life. This was the closest she had ever been, alone, to a man who was not a member of her own family. Even her meetings with her fiancé, Prince Mahail of the neighboring island, had been very formal and closely chaperoned.

"Ronan," he said, and then had to swerve to miss a woman hauling a basket of chickens on her bicycle. He said a delicious-sounding word that she had never heard before, even though she considered her English superb. The little shiver that went up and down her spine told her the word was naughty. Very naughty.

"Ronan." She tried it out, liked how it felt on her tongue. "You must call me Shoshauna!"

"Your Highness, I am not calling you Shoshauna." He muttered the name of a deity under his breath. "I think it's thirty lashes for calling a member of the royal family by their first name."

"Ridiculous," she told him, even though it was true: no one but members of her immediate family would even dare being so familiar as to call her by her first name. That was part of the prison of her role as a member of B'Ranasha's royal family.

But she'd been rescued! Her prayers had been answered just when she had thought there was no hope left, when she had resigned herself to the fact she had agreed to a marriage to a man she did not love.

She did not know how long this reprieve could possibly last, but despite Ronan telling her so sternly this was not a game, Shoshauna intended to make the very most of it. Whether she had been given a few hours or a few days, she intended to be what she might never be again. Free. To be what she had always wanted most to be.

An ordinary girl. With an ordinary life.

She was determined to get a conversation

going, to find out as much about this intriguing foreigner as she could. She glanced at his lips and shivered. Would making the most of the gift the universe had handed her include tasting the lips of the intriguing foreigner?

She knew how *wrong* those thoughts were, but her heart beat faster at the thought. How was it that imagining kissing Ronan, a stranger, could fill her with such delirious curiosity, when the thought of what was supposed to have happened tonight, between her and the man who should have become her husband, Prince Mahail, filled her with nothing but dread?

"What nationality are you?"

"Does it matter? You don't have to know anything about me. You just have to listen to me."

His tone, hard and cold, did not sound promising in the kiss department! Miffed, she wondered how he couldn't know that when a princess asked you something, you did not have the option of not answering. Even though she desperately wanted to try life as an ordinary girl, old habit made her give him her most autocratic stare, the one reserved for misbehaving servants.

"Australian," he snapped.

That explained the accent, surely as delicious sounding as the foreign phrase he had uttered so emphatically when dodging the chicken bicycle. She said the word herself, out loud, using the same inflection he had.

The car swerved, but he regained control instantly. "Don't say that word!" he snapped at her, and then added, a reluctant afterthought at best, "Your Highness."

"I'm trying to improve my English!"

"What you're trying to do is get me a one-way ticket to a whipping post for teaching the princess curse words. Do they still whip people here?"

"Of course," she lied sweetly. His expression darkened to thunder, but then he looked hard at her, read the lie, knew she was having a little fun at his expense. He made a cynical sound deep in his throat.

"Are women in Australia ever forced to marry

men they don't love?" she asked. But the truth was, she had not been *forced*. Not technically. Her father had given her a choice, but it had not been a *real* choice. The weight of his expectation, her own desperate desire to please him, to be of *value* to him had influenced her decision.

Plus, Prince Mahail's surprise proposal had been presented at a low point in her life, just days after her cat, Retnuh, had died.

People said it was just a cat, had been shocked at her level of despair, but she'd had Retnuh since he was a kitten, since she'd been a little girl of eight. He'd been her friend, her companion, her confidante, in a royal household that was too busy to address the needs of one insignificant and lonely little princess.

"Turn here, there's a market down this road."

He took the right, hard, then looked straight ahead.

"Well?" she asked, when it seemed he planned to ignore her.

"People get married all over the world, for all

kinds of reasons," he said. "Love is no guarantee of success. Who even knows what love is?"

"I do," she said stubbornly. It seemed her vision of what it was had crystallized after she'd agreed to marry the completely wrong man. But by then it had been too late. In her eagerness to outrun how terrible she felt about her cat, Shoshauna had allowed herself to get totally caught up in the excitement—preparations underway, two islands celebrating, tailors in overtime preparing gowns for all members of both wedding parties, caterers in overdrive, gifts arriving from all over the world—of getting ready for a royal wedding.

She could just picture the look of abject disappointment on her father's face if she had gone to him and asked to back out.

"Sure you do, Princess."

His tone insinuated she thought love was a storybook notion, a schoolgirl's dream.

"You think I'm silly and immature because I believe in love," she said, annoyed.

"I don't know the first thing about you, what you believe or don't believe. And I don't want to. I have a job to do. A mission. It's to keep you safe. The less I know about you *personally* the better."

Shoshauna felt stunned by that. She was used to interest. Fawning. She could count on no one to tell her what they really thought. Of course, it was all that patently insincere admiration that had made her curl up with her cat at night, listen to his deep purring and feel as if he was the only one who truly got her, who truly loved her for exactly what she was.

If even one person had expressed doubt about her upcoming wedding would she have found the courage to call it off? Instead, she'd been swept along by all that gushing about how wonderful she would look in the dress, how handsome Prince Mahail was, what an excellent menu choice she had made, how exquisite the flowers she had personally picked out.

"There's the market," she said coldly.

He pulled over, stopped her as she reached for the handle. "You are staying right here."

Her arm tingled where his hand rested on it. Unless she was mistaken, he felt a little jolt, too. He certainly pulled away as though he had. "Do you understand? Stay here. Duck down if anyone comes down the road."

She nodded, but perhaps not sincerely enough.

"It's not a game," he said again.

"All right!" she said. "I get it."

"I hope so," he muttered, gave her one long, hard, assessing look, then dashed across the street.

"Don't forget scissors," she called as he went into the market. He glared back at her, annoyed. He hadn't said to be quiet! Besides, she didn't want him to forget the scissors.

She had wanted to cut her hair since she was thirteen. It was too long and a terrible nuisance. It took two servants to wash it and forever to dry.

"Princesses," her mother had informed her, astounded at her request, "do not cut their hair."

Princesses didn't do a great many things. People

who thought it was fun should try it for a day or two. They should try sitting nicely through concerts, building openings, ceremonies for visiting dignitaries. They should try shaking hands with every single person in a receiving line and smiling for hours without stopping. They should try sitting through speeches at formal dinners, being the royal representative at the carefully selected weddings and funerals and baptisms and graduations of the *important* people. They should try meeting a million people and never really getting to know a single one of them.

Shoshauna had dreams that were not princess dreams at all. They were not even big dreams by the standards of the rest of the world, but they were her dreams. And if Ronan thought she wasn't taking what had happened at the chapel seriously, he just didn't get it.

She had given up on her dreams, felt as if they were being crushed like glass under her slippers with every step closer to the altar that she had taken.

But for some reason—maybe she had wished

hard enough after all, maybe Retnuh was her protector from another world—she had been given this reprieve, and she felt as if she had to try and squeeze everything she had ever wanted into this tiny window of freedom.

She wanted to wear pants and shorts. She wanted to ride a motorcycle! She wanted to try surfing and a real bathing suit, not the swimming costume she was forced to wear at the palace. A person could drown if they ever got in real water, not a shallow swimming pool, in that getup.

There were other dreams that were surely never going to happen once she was married to the crown prince of an island country every bit as old-fashioned and traditional as B'Ranasha.

Decorum would be everything. She would wear the finest gowns, the best jewels, her manners would have to be forever impeccable, she would never be able to say what she really wanted. In short order she would be expected to stay home and begin producing babies.

But she wanted so desperately to sample life

before she was condemned to that. Shoshauna wanted to taste snow. She wanted to go on a toboggan. She felt she had missed something essential: a boyfriend, like she had seen in movies. A boyfriend would be fun—someone to hold her hand, take her to movies, romance her. A husband was a totally different thing!

For a moment she had hoped she could talk Ronan into a least pretending, but she now saw that was unlikely.

Most of her dreams were unlikely.

Still, a miracle had happened. Here she was beside a handsome stranger in a stolen taxicab, when she should have been married to Prince Mahail by now. She'd known the prince since childhood and did not find him the least romantic, though many others did, including her silly cousin, Mirassa.

Mahail was absurdly arrogant, sure in his position of male superiority. Worse, he did not believe in her greatest dream of all.

Most of all, Shoshauna wanted to be educated,

to learn glorious things, and not be restricted in what she was allowed to select for course material. She wanted to sit in classrooms with males and openly challenge the stupidity of their opinions. She wanted to learn to play chess, a game her mother said was for men only.

She knew herself to be a princess of very little consequence, the only daughter of a lesser wife, flying well under the radar of the royal watch-dogs. She had spent a great deal of time, especially in her younger years, with her English grandfather and had thought one day she would study at a university in Great Britain.

With freedom that close, with her dreams so near she could taste them, Prince Mahail had spoiled it all, by choosing her as his bride. Why had he chosen her?

Mirassa had told her he'd been captivated by her hair! Suddenly she remembered how Mirassa had looked at her hair in that moment, how her eyes had darkened to black, and Shoshauna felt a shiver of apprehension.

Before Mahail had proposed to Shoshauna, rumor had flown that Mirassa was his chosen bride. He had flirted openly with her on several occasions, which on these islands was akin to publishing banns. Shoshauna had heard, again through the rumor mill, that Mirassa had asked to see him after he had proposed to Shoshauna and he had humiliated her by refusing her an appointment. Given that he had encouraged Mirassa's affection in the first place, he certainly could have been more sensitive. Just how angry had Mirassa been?

Trust your instincts.

If she managed to cut her hair off before her return maybe Prince Mahail would lose interest in her as quickly as he had gained it and Mirassa would stop being jealous.

Being chosen for her hair was insulting, like being a head of livestock chosen for the way it looked: not for its heart or mind or soul!

The prince had taken his interest to her father, and she had felt as if her father had noticed her, *really* seen her for the very first time. His approval had been drugging. It had made her say yes when she had needed to say no!

Ronan came back to the car, dropped a bag on her lap, reached in and stowed a few more on the backseat. She noticed he had purchased clothing for himself and had changed out of the suit he'd worn. He was now wearing an open-throated shirt that showed his arms: rippling with well-defined muscle, peppered with hairs turned golden by the sun. And he was wearing shorts. She was not sure she had ever seen such a length of appealing male leg in all her life!

Faintly flustered, Shoshauna focused on the bag he'd given her. It held clothing. A large pair of very ugly sunglasses, a hideous hat, a blouse and skirt that looked like a British schoolmarm would be happy to wear.

No shorts. She felt like crying as reality collided with her fantasy.

"Where are the scissors?" she asked.

"Forgot," he said brusquely, and she knew she

could not count on him to make any of her dreams come true, to help her make the best use of this time she had been given.

He had a totally different agenda than her. To keep her safe. The last thing she wanted was to be safe. She wanted to be *alive* but in the best sense of that word.

She opened her car door.

"Where the hell are you going?"

"I'm going the *hell* in those bushes, changing into this outfit, as hideous as it is."

"I don't think princesses are supposed to change their clothes in the bushes," he said. "Or say *hell,* for that matter. Just get in the car and I'll find—"

"I'm changing now." *And then I'm going into that market and buying some things I want to wear.* "And then I'm going into that market and finding the restroom."

"Maybe since you're in the bushes anyway, you could just—"

She stopped him with a look. His mouth

snapped shut. He scowled at her, but even he, as unimpressed with her status as he apparently was, was not going to suggest she go to the bathroom in the bushes.

"Don't peek," she said, ducking into the thick shrubbery at the side of the road.

"Lord have mercy," he muttered, whatever that meant.

CHAPTER TWO

RESIGNED, Ronan hovered in front of the bushes while she changed, trying to ignore the rustling sound of falling silk.

When she emerged, even he was impressed with how good his choices had been. Princess Shoshauna no longer looked like a member of the royal family, or even like a native to the island.

The women of B'Ranasha had gorgeous hair, their crowning glory. It swung straight and long, black and impossibly shiny past their shoulder blades, and was sometimes ornamented with fresh flowers, but never hidden.

The princess had managed to tuck her abundant locks up under that straw hat, the sunglasses covered the distinctive turquoise of those eyes, and she'd been entirely correct about his fashion sense.

The outfit he'd picked for her looked hideous in exactly the nondescript way he had hoped it would. The blouse was too big, the skirt was shapeless and dowdy, hanging a nice inch or so past her shapely knees. Except for the delicate slippers that showed off the daintiness of her tiny feet, she could have passed for an over-weight British nanny on vacation.

As a disguise it was perfect: it hid who she really was very effectively. It worked for him, too. He had effectively covered her curves, made her look about as sexy as a refrigerator box. He knew the last thing he needed was to be too aware of her as a woman, and a beautiful one at that.

He accompanied her across the street, thankful for the sleepiness of the market at this time of day. "Try not to talk to anyone. The washrooms are at the back."

His cell phone vibrated. "Five minutes," he told her, checked the caller ID, felt relieved it was not his mother, though not a number he recognized, either. He watched through the open market door as she went straight to the back, then, certain of her safety, turned his attention to the phone.

"Yeah," he said cautiously, not giving away his identity.

"Peterson."

"That's what I figured."

"How did Aurora take the news that she's going to have to go into hiding?"

"Happily waiting for her prince to come," he said dryly, though he thought a less-true statement had probably never been spoken.

"Can you keep her that way for Neptune?"

Neptune was an exercise that Excalibur went on once a year. It was a week-long training in sea operations. Ronan drew in his breath sharply. A week? Even with the cleverness of the disguise she was in, that was going to be tough on so many levels. He didn't know the island. Still, Gray would never ask a week of him if he didn't absolutely need the time.

Surely the princess would know enough about the island to help him figure out a nice quiet place where they could hole up for a week?

Which brought him to how tough it was going to be on another level: a man and a woman holed up alone for a week. A gorgeous woman, despite the disguise, a healthy man, despite all his discipline.

"Can do." He let none of the doubt he was feeling creep into his tone. He hoped the colonel would at least suggest where, but then realized it would be better if he didn't, considering the possibility Gray's team was not secure.

"We'll meet at Harry's. Neptune swim."

Harry's was a fish-and-chips-style pub the guys had frequented near Excalibur headquarters. The colonel was wisely using references no one but a member of the unit would understand. The Neptune swim was a grueling session in ocean swimming that happened at precisely 1500 hours every single day of the Neptune exercise. So, Ronan would meet Gray in one week, at a British-style pub, or a place that sold

fish and chips, presumably close to the palace
headquarters at 3 p.m.

"Gotcha." He deliberately did not use commu-
nication protocol. "By the way, you need to
check out a cousin. Mirassa."

"Thanks. Destroy the phone," the Colonel said.

Every cell phone had a global positioning device
in it. Better to get rid of it, something Ronan had
known all along he was going to have to do.

"Will do."

He hung up the phone and peered in the
market. The princess had emerged from the
back, and was now going through racks of tourist
clothing, in a leisurely manner, hangers of
clothing already tossed over one arm.
Thankfully, despite the darkness of the shop, she
still had on the sunglasses.

He went into the shop, moved through the clut-
tered aisles toward her. If he was not mistaken,
the top item of the clothing she had strung over
her arm was a bikini, bright neon green, not
enough material in it to make a handkerchief.

A week with that? He was disciplined, yes, a miracle worker, no. This was going to be a challenging enough assignment if he managed to keep her dressed like a refrigerator box!

He went up beside her, plucked the bikini off her arm, hung it up on the closest rack. "We're not supposed to attract attention, Aurora. That doesn't exactly fit the bill."

"Aurora?"

"Your code name," he said in an undertone.

"A code name," she breathed. "I like it. Does it mean something?"

"It's the name of the princess in 'Sleeping Beauty.'"

"Well, I'm not waiting for my prince!"

"I gathered that," he said dryly. He didn't want to feel interested in what was wrong with her prince. It didn't have anything to do with getting the job done. He told himself not to ask her why she dreaded marriage so much, and succeeded, for the moment. But he was aware he had a whole week with her to try to keep his curiosity at bay.

"Do you have a code name?" she asked.

He tried to think of the name of a celibate priest, but he wasn't really up on his priests. "No. Let's go."

She glanced at him—hard to read her eyes through the sunglasses—but her chin tilted in a manner that did not bode well for him being the boss. She took the bikini back off the rack, tossed it back over her arm.

"I don't have to wear it," she said mulishly. "I just have to have it. Touch it again, and I'll make a scene." She smiled.

He glanced around uneasily. No other customers in the store, the single clerk, thankfully, far more interested in the daily racing form he was studying than he was in them.

"Let's go," he said in a low voice. "You have enough stuff there to last a year."

"Maybe it will be a year," she said, just a trifle too hopefully, confirming what he already knew—this was one princess not too eager to be kissed by a prince.

"I've had some instructions. A week. We need to disappear for a week."

She grabbed a pair of shorty-shorts.

"We have to go."

"I'm not finished."

He took her elbow, glanced again at the clerk, guided her further back in the room. "Look, Princess, you have a decision to make."

She spotted a bikini on the rack by his head. "I know!" she said, deliberately missing his point. "Pink or green?"

Definitely pink, but he forced himself to remain absolutely expressionless, pretended he was capable of ignoring the scrap of material she was waving in front of his face. Unfortunately, it was just a little too easy to imagine her in that, how the pink would set off the golden tones of her skin and the color of her eyes, how her long black hair would shimmer against it.

He took a deep breath.

"This is about your life," he told her quietly. "Not mine. I'm not going to be more responsible for you than you are willing to be for yourself. So, if you want to take chances with your life, if you want to make my life difficult instead of cooperating, I'll take you back to the palace right now."

Despite the sunglasses, he could tell by the tightening of her mouth that she didn't want to go back to the palace, so he pressed on.

"That would work better for me, actually," he said. "I kind of fell into this. I signed up for wedding security, not to be your bodyguard. I have a commanding officer who's going to be very unhappy with me if I don't report back to work on Tuesday."

He was bluffing. He wasn't taking her back to the palace until Gray had sorted out who was responsible for the attack at the church. And Gray would look after getting word back to his unit that he had been detained due to circumstances beyond his control.

But she didn't have to know that. And if he'd read her correctly, she'd been relieved that her wedding had been interrupted, delirious almost. The last thing she wanted to do was go back to her life, pick up where she'd left off.

He kept talking. "I'm sure your betrothed is very worried about you, anxious to make you his wife, so that he can keep you safe. He's probably way more qualified to do that than I am."

He could see, *clearly,* that he had her full attention, and that she was about as eager to get back to her prince as to swim with crocodiles.

So he said, "Maybe that's the best idea. Head back, a quick secret ceremony, you and your prince can get off the island, have your honeymoon together, and this whole mess will be cleared up by the time you get home."

His alertness to detail paid off now, because her body language radiated sudden tension. He actually felt a little bit sorry for her. She obviously didn't want to get married, and if she had feelings for her fiancé they were not positive ones. But again he had to shut down any sense of curiosity or compassion that he felt. That wasn't his problem, and in protection work, that was the priority: to remember his business—the very narrow perimeters of keeping her safe—and to not care anything about what was her business.

Whether she was gorgeous, ugly, unhappy at love, frustrated with her life, none of that mattered to him. Or should matter to him.

Still, he did feel the tiniest little shiver of unwanted sympathy as he watched her getting paler before his eyes. He was glad for her sunglasses, because he didn't want to see her eyes just now. She put the pink bikini back, thankfully, but turned and marched to the counter as if she was still the one in charge, as if he was her servant left to trail behind her—and pay the bills.

Apparently paying had not occurred to her. She had probably never had to handle money or even a credit card in her whole life. She would put it on account, or some member of her staff would look after the details for her.

She seemed to realize that at the counter, and he could have embarrassed her, but there was no point, and he certainly did not want the clerk to find anything memorable about this transaction.

"I got it, sweetheart," he said easily.

Though playing sweethearts had been her idea, she was flustered by it. She looked everywhere but at him. Then, without warning, she reached up on tiptoe and kissed him on the cheek.

"Thanks, Charming," she said huskily, obviously deciding he needed a code name that matched hers.

But a less-likely prince had never been born, and he knew it.

He hoped the clerk wouldn't look up, because there might be something memorable about seeing a man blushing because his supposed lady friend had kissed him and used an odd endearment on him.

Ronan didn't make it worse by looking at her, but he felt a little stunned by the sweetness of her lips on his cheek, by the utter softness, the sensuality of a butterfly's wings.

"Oh, look," she said softly, suddenly breathless. She was tapping a worn sign underneath the glass on the counter.

"Motorcycles for rent. Hour, day, week."

It would be the last time he'd be able to use this credit card, so maybe, despite his earlier rejection of the idea, now was the time to change vehicles. Was it a genuinely good idea or had that spontaneous kiss on the cheek rattled him?

He'd already nixed the motorcycle idea in his own mind. Why was he revisiting the decision?

Was he losing his edge? Finding her just too distracting? He had to do his job, to make decisions based solely on what was most likely to bring him to mission success, which was keeping her safe. Getting stopped in a stolen car was not going to do that. Blending in with the thousands of tourists that scootered around this island made more sense.

Since talking to Gray, he wondered if the whole point of the threats against the princess had been to stop the wedding, not harm her personally.

But he knew he couldn't let his guard down

because of that. He had to treat the threat to her safety as real, or there would be too many temptations to treat it lightly, to let his guard down, to let her get away with things.

"Please?" she said softly, and then she tilted her sunglasses down and looked at him over the rims.

Her eyes were stunning, the color and depth of tropical waters, filled at this moment with very real pleading, as if she felt her life depended on getting on that motorcycle.

Half an hour later, he had a backpack filled with their belongings, he had moved the car off the road into the thick shrubs beside it and he was studying the motorcycle. It was more like a scooter than a true motorcycle.

He took a helmet from a rack beside the motorcycles.

"Come here."

"I don't want to wear that! I want to feel the wind in my hair."

He had noticed hardly anyone on the island did wear motorcycle helmets, probably because the top speed of these little scooters would be about eighty kilometers an hour. Still, acquiring the motorcycle felt a bit like giving in, and he was done with that. His job was to keep her safe in every situation. Life could be cruelly ironic, he knew. It would be terrible to protect her from an assassin and then get her injured on a motorbike.

"Please, Charming?" she said.

That had worked so well last time, she was already trying it again! It served him right for allowing himself to be manipulated by her considerable charm.

She took off her sunglasses and blinked at him. He could see the genuine yearning in her eyes, but knew he couldn't cave in. This was a girl who was, no doubt, very accustomed to people jumping to make her happy, to wrapping the whole world around her pinky finger.

"Charming isn't a good code name for me," he said.

"Why not?"

"Because I'm not. Charming. And I'm certainly not a prince." To prove both, he added, sternly, "Now, come here and put on the helmet."

"Are you wearing one?"

He didn't answer, just lifted his eyebrow at her, the message clear. She could put on the helmet or she could go home.

Mutinously she snatched the straw hat from her head.

He tried not to let his shock show. In those few unsupervised minutes while he had talked to Gray on the phone, she had gone to the washroom, all right, but not for the reason he had thought or she had led him to believe. Where had she gotten her hands on a pair of scissors? Or maybe, given the raggedness of the cut, she had used a knife.

She was no hairdresser, either. Little chunks of her black hair stood straight up on her head, going every which way. The bangs were crooked. Her ears were tufted. There wasn't a place where her hair was more than an inch and a half long. Her head looked like a newly hatched chicken, covered in dark dandelion fluff. It should have looked tragic.

Instead, she looked adorable, carefree and elfish, a rebel, completely at odds with the conservative outfit he had picked for her. Without the distraction of her gorgeous hair, it was apparent that her bone structure was absolutely exquisite, her eyes huge, her lips full and puffy.

"Where's your hair?" he asked, fighting hard not to let his shock show. He shoved the helmet on her head quickly, before she had any idea how disconcerting he found her new look. His fingers fumbled on the strap buckle, he was way too aware of her, and not at all pleased with his awareness. The perfume he'd caught a whiff of at the wedding tickled his nostrils.

"I cut it."

"I can clearly see that." Thankfully, the mysteries of the helmet buckle unraveled, he tightened the strap, let his hands fall away. He was relieved the adorable mess of her hair was covered. "What did you do with it after you cut it?"

Her contrite expression told him she had left it where it had fallen.

"So, you did it for nothing," he said sternly. "Now, when we're traced this far, and we will be, they'll find out you cut your hair. And they'll be looking for a bald girl, easier to spot than you were before."

"I'm not bald," she protested.

"I've seen better haircuts on new recruits," he said. She looked crestfallen, he told himself he didn't care. But he was aware he did, just a little bit.

"I'll go back and pick up my hair," she said.

"Never mind. Hopefully no one is going to see you."

"Does it look that bad?"

He could reassure her it didn't, but that was something Prince Charming might do. "It looks terrible."

He hoped she wasn't going to cry. She put her sunglasses back on a little too rapidly. Her shoulders trembled tellingly.

Don't be a jerk, he told himself. But then he realized he might be a lot safer in this situation if she did think he was a jerk.

When had his focus switched from her safety to his own?

Rattled, he pushed ahead. "I need you to think very carefully," he said. "Is there a place on this island we can go where no one would find us for a week?"

He tried not to close his eyes after he said it. A week with her, her new haircut and her new green bikini stuffed in the backpack. Not to mention the shorty-shorts, and a halter top that had somehow been among her purchases.

He could see in her eyes she yearned for things that were forbidden to her, things she might not even be totally aware of, things that went far beyond riding on motorcycles and cutting her hair.

Things her husband should be teaching her. Right this minute. He had no right to be feeling grateful that she had not been delivered into the hands of a man she'd dreaded discovering those things with.

Instead she'd been delivered into his hands. One mission: keep her safe. Even from himself.

Still, he was aware he was a warrior, not a saint. The universe was asking way too much of him.

He turned from her swiftly, got on the motor-cycle, persuaded it to life. He patted the seat behind him, not even looking at her.

But not looking at her didn't help. She slid onto the seat behind him. The skirt hiked way up. Out of his peripheral vision he could see the nak-edness of her knee. He glanced back. The skirt was riding high up her thigh.

It was a princess like no one had ever seen, of that he was certain. On the other hand, no one would be likely to recognize her looking like this, either.

"Hang on tight," he said.

And then he felt her sweet curves pull hard against him. Oh, sure. For once she was going to listen!

"I know a place," she called into his ear. "I know the perfect place."

His cell phone vibrated in his pocket. He slowed, checked the caller ID. His mother. He wrestled an impulse to answer, to yell at her, Don't do it! Instead he listened to her leave yet another voice mail.

"Ronan, call me. It's so exciting."

They were crossing over a bridge, rushing water below, and he took the phone and flung it into the water.

He was in the protection business; sometimes it felt as if the whole world was his responsibility. But the truth was he could not now, and never had been able to, protect his own mother from what she most needed protecting from.

Herself.

Shoshauna pressed her cheek up against the delicious hardness of Ronan's shoulder. His scent, soapy and masculine, was stronger than the scent of the new shirt.

Alone with him for a week. In a place where no one could find them. It felt dangerous and exciting and terribly frightening, too. She pressed into him, feeling far more endangered than she had when the gun had gone off in the chapel.

Some kind of trembling had started inside her, and it was not totally because he had hurt her feelings telling her her hair looked terrible. It wasn't totally because of the vibration of the motorbike, either!

"Go faster," she cried.

He glanced over his shoulder at her.

"It doesn't go any faster," he shouted back at her, but he gave it a hit of gas and the little bike surged forward.

Her stomach dropped, and she squealed with delight.

He glanced back again. His lips were twitching. He was trying not to smile. But he did, and his smile was like the sun coming out on the grayest of days. That glimpse of a smile made her forget she had only a short time to squeeze many dreams into, though a week was more than she could have hoped for.

Still, it was as if his smile hypnotized her and made her realize maybe there was one dream he could help make come true. A dream more important than wearing shorts or riding astride or touching snow. A dream that scorned people who pretended all the time.

She had only a few days, and she wanted to be with someone who was real, not kowtowing. Not anxious to please. Not afraid of her position. Someone who would tell her the truth, even if it hurt to hear it.

I'm not going to be more responsible for you than you are willing to be for yourself, he had told her. She shivered. In that simple statement, as much as it had pained her to hear it, was the truth about how her life had gone off track so badly. Could Ronan somehow lead her back to what was real about herself?

When she was younger, there'd been a place she had been allowed to go where she had felt real. Relaxed. As if it was okay to be herself.

Herself—something more and more lost

behind the royal mask, the essential facades of good manners, of duty. Something that might be lost forever when she was returned to Prince Mahail as his bride.

"There's an island," she called over the putter of the engine. "My grandparents have a summer place on a small island just north of the mainland. No one is ever there at this time of year."

"No one? No security? No groundskeeper?"

"It's a private island, but not the posh kind. You'd have to know my grandfather to understand. He hates all the royal fuss-fuss as he calls it. He likes simplicity.

"The island is almost primitive. There's no electricity, the house is like a cottage, it even has a thatched roof."

"Fresh water, or do we have to bring our own?"

"There's a stream." Ronan thought like a soldier, she realized. All she could think about was it would be such a good place to try on her new bikini, such a wonderful place to rediscover who she really was! But, given the strange trembling inside her, how wise would that be? Given the reality of his smile, the pure sexiness of it, was it possible she was headed into a worse danger zone than the one she was leaving?

"Bedding? Blankets?"

His mind, thankfully, a million miles from bikinis, on the more practical considerations. "I think so."

"How do you get to it?"

"My grandfather keeps a boat at the dock across the bay from it."

"Perfect," he said. "Show me the fastest way to the boat dock."

But she didn't tell him the shortest way. She directed him the longest way possible, because who knew if she would ever ride a motorcycle again, her arms wrapped so intimately around a man with such an incredible, sexy smile?

She *loved* the motorcycle, even if she had been deprived of feeling the fingers of the wind playing with her hair. She could still feel the island breeze on her face, playing with the hem of her skirt, touching her legs. She could feel the kiss of warm sunshine. She had a lovely sensation of being connected to everything around her. The air was perfumed, birds and monkeys chattered in the trees. She didn't feel separate from it, she felt like a part of it.

And she could feel the exquisite sensation of being connected to him—her arms wrapped around the hard-muscled bands of his stomach, her cheek resting on the solid expanse of his back, her legs forming a rather intimate vee around him.

Her mother, she knew, would have an absolute fit. And her father wouldn't be too happy with her, either. She could only imagine how Mahail would feel if he saw her now!

Which only added to the delectable sense of dancing with danger that Princess Shoshauna was feeling: free, adventurous, as if anything at all could happen.

Just this morning her whole life had seemed to be mapped out in front of her, her fate inescapable. Now she had hair that Prince Mahail would hate, and she didn't think he'd like it very much that she had spent a week alone with a strange man, either!

"Can you go faster?' she called to Ronan over the wind.

The slightest hesitation, and then he did, opening the bike up so that they were roaring down the twisting highway, until tears formed in her eyes and she could feel the thrill to the bottom of her belly.

She refused to dwell on how long it would last, or if this was the only time she would ever do this.

Instead she threw back her head and laughed out loud for the sheer joy of the moment, at her unexpected encounter with the most heady drug of all—freedom.

CHAPTER THREE

RONAN cut the engine of the motorboat, letting it drift in to the deserted beach. He glanced at the princess, asleep in the bottom of the boat, exhausted from the day, and decided there was no need for both of them to get wet. He stood up, stepped off the hull into a gentle surf. The seawater was warm on his legs as he dragged the boat up onto the sand.

It was night, but the sky was breathtaking, starstudded. A full moon frosted each softly lapping wave in white and painted the fine beach sand a bewitching shade of silver.

From a soldier's perspective, the island was perfect. Looking back across the water, he could barely make out the dark outline of the main island of B'Ranasha. He could see the odd light flickering on that distant shore.

He had circled this island once in the boat, a rough reconnaissance. It was only about eight kilometers all the way around it. Better yet, it had only this one protected bay, and only the one beach suitable for landing a boat.

Everywhere else the thick tropical growth, or rocky cliffs, came right to the water's edge. The island was too small and bushed in to land a plane on. It would be a nightmare to parachute in to, and it would be a challenge to land a helicopter here. Planes and helicopters gave plenty of warning they were arriving, anyway.

It was a highly defensible position. Perfect from a soldier's perspective.

But from a personal point of view, from a man's perspective, it couldn't be much worse. It was a deserted island more amazing than a movie set. The sand was white, fine and flawless, exotic birds filled the night air with music, a tantalizing perfume rode the gentle night breeze. Palm trees swayed in the wind, ferns and flowers abounded.

At the head of the beach was a cottage, palm-frond roof, screened porch looking out to the sea. It was the kind of retreat people came to on holidays and honeymoons, not to hide out. Which was a good thing. He highly doubted anyone would think to look for the princess here.

He gave the rope attached to the boat another pull, hauled it further up on the sand until he was satisfied it would be safe, even from the tide, which, according to the tide charts he had purchased at a small seaside village, would come up during the night.

Only then did he peer back at Aurora, his very own Sleeping Beauty. The princess, worn down from all the unscheduled excitement of her wedding day, was curled up in the bottom of the boat, fast asleep on a bed of life jackets.

The silver of the moon washed her in magic, though he felt the shock of her shorn head again, followed by a jolt of a different kind—the short hair did nothing but accentuate her loveliness. Right now he was astonished by the length and fullness of her lashes, casting sooty shadows on the roundness of her cheeks. Her lips moved, forming words in her sleep, something in her own language, *ret-nuh.*

He'd insisted on a life jacket, but the skirt was riding high up her legs, he caught a glimpse of bridal white panties so pure he could feel a certain dryness in his mouth. He reached out and gave the skirt a tug down, whether to save her embarrassment or to save himself he wasn't quite sure.

A deserted island. A beautiful woman. A week. He was no math whiz, but he knew a bad equation when he came across it.

He'd done plenty of protection duty, and though it wasn't his favorite assignment, Ronan prided himself on doing his work well. He'd protected heads of states and their families, politicians, royalty, CEOs.

The person being protected was known

amongst the team as the "principal." The team didn't even use personal names when they discussed strategy, formulated plans. The cardinal rule, the constant in protection work, was maintaining a completely professional, arm's-length relationship. Emotional engagement compromised the mission, period.

But the very circumstances of those other assignments made maintaining professionalism easy. The idea of forming any kind of deeper relationship or even a friendship, with the principal had been unthinkable. There was always a team, never just one person. There was always an environment conducive to maintaining preordained boundaries.

Ronan was in brand-new territory, and he didn't like it. So, before he woke her up, he looked to the stars, gathered his strength, reminded himself of the mission, the boundaries, the *rules*.

"Hey," he called softly, finally, "wake up."

She stirred but didn't wake, and he leaned into

the boat and nudged her shoulder with his hand. She was slender as a reed, the roundness of her shoulder the epitome of feminine softness.

"Princess." It would be infinitely easy to reach in and scoop her up, to carry her across the sand to that cottage, but that brief contact with her shoulder was fair warning it would be better not to add one little bit of physical contact to the already volatile combination.

A bad time to think of her lips on his cheek earlier in the day, her slight curves pressed hard against him on that motorcycle.

"Wake up," he said louder, more roughly.

She did, blinked—that blank look of one who couldn't quite place where they were. And then she focused on him and smiled in a way that could melt even the most professional soldier's dedication to absolute duty.

She sat up, looked around and then sighed with contentment. She liked being here. She had liked the entire day way too much! He had not been nearly as immune to her laughter and her arms wrapped around him as he had wanted to be, but thankfully she didn't have to know that!

She shrugged out of the life jacket and then stretched, pressing the full sensuous roundness of her breasts into the thin fabric of the ill-fitting blouse. Then she stood up. The boat rocked on the sand, and the physical contact he wanted so badly not to happen, happened anyway. He caught her, steadied her as the boat rocked on the uneven ground. She took one more step, the boat pitched, and she would have gone to her knees.

Except his hands encircled her waist nearly completely, the thumb and index finger of his right hand nearly touching those of his left. He lifted her from the boat, swung her onto the sand, amazed by her slightness. She didn't weigh any more than a fully loaded combat pack.

"You're strong!" she said.

He withdrew from her swiftly, not allowing himself to preen under her admiration. A week. They had to make it a week.

"It's beautiful, isn't it?" she asked, hugging

herself, apparently oblivious to his discomfort. "I love it here. My grandfather called it Naidina Karobin—it means something like *my heart is home.*"

Great.

"Isn't that pretty?"

"Yeah, sure." Real men didn't use words like *pretty.* Except maybe in secret, when they looked at a face like hers, washed in moonlight, alive with discovery. *Mission.*

He reached into the boat and grabbed the knapsack. As he followed her across the sand toward the cottage, he noted that the trees in the grove around it were loaded with edible fruits, coconuts, bananas, mangos.

He'd landed in the Garden of Eden. He only hoped he could resist the apple. *Boundaries.*

As they got closer, the princess jacked her skirt up and ran, danced really, across the sand. She looked like some kind of moonlit nymph, her slender legs painted in silver. *Rules, duty, professionalism.*

He followed her more slowly, as if he could put off the moment when they set up housekeeping together and everything intensified yet more.

Becoming part of Excalibur, Ronan's endurance, physical strength, intellectual assets, ability to cope with stress had all been tested beyond normal limits. One man in twenty who was recruited for that unit made it through the selection process. Membership meant being stronger, faster, tougher in mind and spirit than the average man.

And yet to share the space of that cottage on this island with a real-live sleeping beauty seemed as if it would test him in ways he had never been tested before.

Ronan had been in possession of the princess for less than twenty-four hours and he already felt plenty tested!

He drew a deep breath as he followed her up wide steps to the screen door that he thought had been a screened-in veranda. As his eyes adjusted to the lack of moonlight inside, he saw he had been mistaken.

It was not a screened porch, but a screened-in house. A summer house, she'd said, obviously designed so that it caught the breeze from every angle on hot summer nights. The huge overhang of the roof would protect it from the rare days of inclement weather these islands experienced.

White, sheer curtains lifted and fell in the breeze, making the inside of the house enchanting and exotic. The main room had dark, beautiful wooden floors, worn smooth from years of use, moonlight spilling across them. Deeply cushioned, colorful rattan furniture was grouped casually around a coffee table, a space that invited conversation, relaxation.

Intimacy.

At the other end of the room was a dining area, the furniture old, dark, exquisitely carved and obviously valuable. That such good furniture would be left out in an unlocked cottage should have reassured him how safe the island was. But Ronan was a little too aware that the dangers here could come from within, not without.

The screens as walls gave a magnificent illusion of there being no separation between the indoor living space and the outdoors.

He spied a hurricane lamp and lit it, hoping the light would chase away the feeling of enchantment, but instead, in the flickering golden light, the great room became downright romantic, soft, sultry, sensual.

The light was soft on her face, too, her expression rapt as she looked around, her eyes glowing with the happiness of memories.

Ronan would have liked it a lot better if she was spoiled rotten, complaining about spiderwebs and the lack of electricity.

To distance himself from the unwanted *whoosh* of attraction he felt, Ronan went hurriedly across the room to investigate a door at the back of it. It led to an outdoor kitchen, and he went out. The outdoor cooking space was complete with a huge wood-fired oven and a grill. Open shelves were lined with canned goods. A person could camp out here, on this island, comfortably, for a year.

Beyond that, in a flower- and fern-encircled grove was an open-air shower, and the *whoosh* he'd been trying to outrun came back.

He reentered the house reluctantly, thankful he didn't see her right away. He finished his inventory of the main house: there were two rooms off the great room, and he entered the first. It was the main bedroom, almost entirely taken up by a huge bed framed with soaring rough timbers, dark with age, more sheer white curtains flowing around the bed, surrounding it. Again the screens acting as outer walls made the bed seem to be set right amongst the palms and mango trees. The perfume of a thousand different flowers tickled his nose. There was no barrier to sound, either. The sea whispered poetry. He backed hastily out of there.

Princess Shoshauna was in the smaller of the bedrooms, looking around and hugging herself.

"This is where I always stayed when I was a child! Look how it feels as if you are right outside! My grandfather designed this house. He was an architect. That's how he came to be on B'Ranasha. I'll have this room."

He would have much preferred she take the bigger room, act snotty and entitled so he could kill the *whoosh* in his stomach.

"I think you should take the bigger room," he suggested. "You are the princess."

"Not this week I'm not." She smiled, delighted to have declared herself not a princess.

If she wasn't a princess, if she was just an ordinary girl…he cut off the train of his thought. It didn't matter if she was a wandering gypsy. She was still the *principal*, and it was still his mission to protect her.

He reached into his pocket, took out a pocket-knife and cut the cord that kept the mattress rolled up. He found the bedding in a tightly closed trunk under the bed. A floral sachet had been packed with it, and the white linen sheets smelled exotic.

He laid them quickly on the bed, then watched, bemused, when she eyed the pile of bedding as though it were an interesting but baffling jigsaw puzzle.

"You don't know how to make a bed," he guessed, incredulous, then wondered why it would surprise him that a princess had no idea how to make a bed.

The truth was, it would be way too easy to forget she was a princess, especially with her standing there with shorn hair, and in a badly rumpled and ill-fitting dress.

But that was exactly what he had to remember, to keep his boundaries clear, his professionalism unsullied, his duty foremost in his mind. She was a princess, a real one. He was a soldier. Their stations in life were millions of miles apart. And they were going to stay that way.

"My mother would never have allowed it," she said, sadly. "She had this idea that to do things that could be done by servants was *common*. Of course, she was a commoner, and she never quite overcame her insecurity about it."

She didn't know how to make a bed.

Every soldier had been tormented, at one time or another, with making a bed that could satisfy a drill sergeant who had no intention of being satisfied. Ronan could make a bed—perfectly—anywhere, anytime.

To focus on the differences between them would strengthen his will. To perceive her as pampered and useless would go a long way in erasing the memory of her slender curves pressed into his back as they rode that motorcycle together.

"I'd be happy to make it for you, Princess," he said.

She glared at him. "I don't want you to make it for me! I want you to show me how to make it."

He was tired. He had not had the benefit of a two hour nap in the bottom of the boat. She had slept for an hour or so before that, as well, while they had waited, hidden, for it to get dark enough to take her grandfather's boat from the dock and cross the water without being seen.

It would be easier for him to make the bed himself, but he had to get through a full week, and that wasn't going to be easy if he argued with her over little things.

His eyes went to the full puffiness of her lips, and he felt his own weariness, his resolve flickering.

He had to get though a full week without kissing her, too.

Making a bed together didn't seem like a very good starting point for keeping things professional and distant. Neither did fighting with her.

He had the uneasy feeling he'd better adjust to being put in no-win positions by the princess.

He separated the sheets from the blankets, found the bottom sheet and tossed it over the mattress.

"First you tuck this under the mattress," he said.

"I'll do it!" she said, when he reached out to demonstrate.

He held up his hands in surrender, stood back, tried not to wince at her sloppy corners, the slack fabric in the center of the bed. He didn't offer to help as she grunted over lifting the corners of the mattress.

He handed her the second sheet, tried to stay

expressionless as she shoved it under the bottom of the mattress in such a bunched-up mess that the mattress lifted.

She caught the tip of her tongue between her teeth as she focused with furious concentration on the task at hand. He folded his arms firmly over his chest.

She inserted the pillows in the cases with the seams in the wrong places and fluffed them. Then he handed her the top blanket, which she tossed haphazardly on top of the rest of her mess.

The bed was a buck private's nightmare, but she smiled with pleasure at her final result. To his eye, it looked more like a nest than a well-made bed.

"See?" she said. "I can do ordinary things."

"Yes," he said, deadpan. "I can clearly see that."

Something in his tone must have betrayed him, because she searched his face with grave suspicion.

A drill sergeant would have had the thrill of ripping it apart and making her do it again, but he wasn't a drill sergeant. In fact, at the moment he was just an ordinary guy, trying to survive.

"Okay," he said, "if you have everything—"

"Oh, I'll make yours, too. For practice."

"What do you need practice making a bed for?" he asked crankily. He didn't want her touching his bedding.

He was suddenly acutely aware of how alone they were here, of how the dampness of the sea air was making the baggy dress cling to her, of how her short hair was curling slightly from humidity, and there seemed to be a dewy film forming on her skin. He was aware of how her tongue had looked, caught between her teeth.

Ignoring him, she marched right by him into his room. He trailed behind her reluctantly, watched as she opened the trunk where the linens were kept and began tossing them on his bed.

"I'm going to do all kinds of ordinary things this week," she announced.

"Such as?" He didn't offer to help her make the bed, just watched, secretly aghast at the mess she was making.

"Cooking!" she decided.

"I can hardly wait."

He got the suspicious look again.

"Washing dishes. Doing laundry. You can show me those things, can't you?"

She sounded so enthused he thought she must be pulling his leg, but he could tell by the genuine eager expression on her face she really wasn't.

How did a man maintain professional distance from a princess who wanted nothing more than to be an ordinary girl, who was enthralled at the prospect of doing the most ordinary of things?

He nodded cautiously.

"I would like to learn how to sew on a button," she decided. "Do you know how to do that?"

Sewing buttons, insignia, pant hems, was right up there with making beds in a soldier's how-to arsenal, but she didn't wait for him to answer.

"And I can't wait to swim in the ocean! I used to swim here when I was a child. I love it!"

He thought of that bikini in their backpack, closed his eyes, marshaling strength.

"You don't happen to know how to surf, do

you?" she asked him. "There used to be a surf-board under the cottage. I hope it's still there!"

His boyhood days had been spent on a surf-board. It was probably what had saved him from delinquency, his love of the waves, his *need* to perfect the dance with the extraordinary, crashing power of them.

"This bay doesn't look like it would ever get much in the way of surf," he told her. "It's pretty protected."

She looked disappointed, but then brightened. "There's snorkeling equipment under there, too. Maybe we can do that."

We, as if they were two kids together on vacation. Now would be the time to let her know he had no intention of being her playmate, but he held his tongue.

She gave his bed a final, satisfied pat. "Well, good night Ronan. I can't wait for tomorrow." She blew him a kiss, which was only slightly better than the one she had planted on his cheek earlier in the day.

He rubbed his cheek, aggravated, as if the kiss had actually landed, an uncomfortably whimsical thought for a man who prided himself on his pragmatic nature. He listened for her to get into her own bed, then went on silent feet and checked each side of the cabin.

The night was silent, except for the night birds. The ocean was dark and still, the only lights were from the moon and stars, the few lights on the mainland had winked out.

He went back into his bedroom. He knew he needed to sleep, that it would help him keep his thinking clear and disciplined. He also knew he had acquired, over the years, that gift peculiar to soldiers of sleeping in a state of readiness. Any sound that didn't belong would awaken him instantly. His highly developed sixth sense would guard them both through the night.

He shrugged out of his shirt but left the shorts on. He certainly didn't want her to ever see him in his underwear, and he might have to get out of bed quickly in the night. He climbed into bed.

It had to be his imagination that her perfume lingered on the sheets. Still, tired as he was, he tossed and turned until finally, an hour later, he got out of the bed, remade it *perfectly*. He got back in and slept instantly.

Shoshauna awoke to light splashing across her bed, birdsong, the smell and sound of the sea.

She remembered she was on her grandfather's island and thought to herself, my heart *is* home. She remembered her narrow escape from marriage, the unexpected gifts yesterday: riding the motorcycle, buying the daring bathing suit and shorty-shorts.

Kissing Ronan on the cheek. Feeling the muscles of his back as they shared the motorcycle, feeling his hands encircle her waist.

Ronan was a gloriously made man, all hard muscle, graceful efficiency of movement, easy, unconscious strength, a certain breathtaking confidence in his physical abilities. Add to that the soft, firm voice, his accent. And his eyes! A soldier's eyes to be sure, stern, forbidding even. But when the mask slipped, when they glinted with laughter, she felt this uncontrollable—and definitely wicked—shiver of pure wanting. He made her feel such an amazing mixture of things: excited and shy, aggravated, annoyed, *alive.*

Shoshauna knew it was wrong to be thinking like that. She was promised to another. And yet…if you could pick a man to spend a week on a deserted island with, you would pick a man like Ronan.

She gave her head a shake at the naughty direction of her own thoughts and realized her head felt unnaturally light and then remembered she had cut her hair.

She had glimpsed her hair in the mirror of the motorcycle. Now she hopped out of bed and had a good look in the mirror above the dressing table.

"Oh!" she said, touching her fingers to it. It looked awful, crushed in places from sleep, standing straight up in others. Despite that, she decided she loved it. It made her look like a girl who would never back down from an adventure, not a princess who had spent her life in a tower, at least figuratively speaking! In fact, she felt in love with life this morning, excited about whatever new gifts the day held. Excited about a chance to get to know Ronan better.

But wasn't that a betrayal of the man she was promised to?

Not necessarily, she told herself. This was her opportunity to be ordinary!

She realized she had not felt this way—happy, hopeful—since she had said yes to Prince Mahail's proposal. Up till now she had woken up each and every morning with a knot in her stomach that shopping for the world's most luxurious trousseau could not begin to undo. She had woken each morning with a growing sense of dread, a prisoner counting down to their date with the gallows.

Her stomach dipped downward, reminding her that her reprieve was probably temporary at best.

But she refused to think of that now, to waste even one precious moment of her freedom.

Ronan had left the backpack in her room, and she pawed through it, found the shorty-shorts and a red, spaghetti-strapped shirt that hugged her curves. She put on the outfit and twirled in front of the mirror, her sense of being an *ordinary* girl increased sweetly.

Her mother would have hated both the amount of leg showing and the skimpiness of the top, which made Shoshauna enjoy her outfit even more. She liked the way lots of bare skin against warm air felt: free, faintly sensual and very comfortable.

She went out her door, saw his bedroom was already empty. She stopped when she saw his bed was made, hesitated, then went in and inspected it. The bedding was crisp and taut. She backed out when she realized the room smelled like him: something so masculine and rich it was nearly drugging.

She went back to her own room, tugged the rumpled bedding into some semblance of order, declared herself and the room perfectly wonderfully ordinary and went in search of Ronan.

He was at the outdoor kitchen, a basket of fruit beside him that he was peeling and cutting into chunks. She watched him for a moment, enjoying the pure poetry of him performing such a simple task, and then blushed when he glanced at her and lifted an eyebrow. He had known she stood there observing him!

Still, there was a flash of something in his eyes as he took in her outfit, before it was quickly veiled, a barrier swiftly erected. And there was no hint of that *flash* in his voice.

"Princess," he said formally, "did you sleep well?"

It was several giant steps back from the man who had laughed with her yesterday. She wanted to break down the barrier she saw in his eyes. What good was being an ordinary girl if it was as if she was on this island alone? If her intrigue with this man was not shared?

"You must call me Shoshauna," she said.

"I can't."

She glared at him. "I command it."

He actually laughed out loud, the same laugh that had given her her first glimpse yesterday of just how real he could be, making her yearn to know him, know someone real.

"Command away, Princess. I'm not calling you by your first name."

"Why?"

"It's too familiar. I'm your bodyguard, not your buddy."

She felt the sting of that. Her disappointment was acute. He wanted the exact opposite of what she wanted! She wanted to feel close to another human being, he wanted to feel distant. She wanted to use this time together to explore his mysteries, he was just as determined to keep them secret.

It was frustrating! Her mother would approve of his attitude, a man who knew his *place* and was so determined to keep their different positions as a barrier between them.

But so would her grandmother love him. Her grandmother said soldiers made the best husbands, because they already knew how to obey. Not that he was showing any sign of obeying Shoshauna!

And not that she wanted to be thinking of this handsome man and the word *husband* in the same sentence. She had just narrowly missed making marriage her fate.

Still, she wanted him to participate in the great adventure she was on. How could she forget she was a princess, forget her obligations and duties for a short while, if he was going to insist on reminding her at every turn by using a formal title?

"How about my code name, then?" she asked.

He hesitated, glanced at her, shrugged. She couldn't tell if it was agreement or appeasement, though whichever it was, she sensed it was a big concession from him, he suddenly refused to look at her, took an avid interest in the fruit in front of him.

"I'll do that," she said, moving up beside him. Did he move a careful step away from her? She moved closer. He moved away again and without looking at her, passed her a little tiny knife and a mango.

"Don't cut your fingers off," he said dryly.

She watched for a moment as his own fingers handled the knife, removed a fine coil of peel from the fruit. He caught her watching him, *again,* put down the knife and turned away from her to put wood in the oven.

"What are we going to make in there?" she asked eagerly.

"*I'm* going to make biscuits."

"I want to learn!"

"What for?"

"It seems like it would be a useful skill," she said stubbornly.

"It is a useful skill. For someone like me, who frequently finds himself trying to make the best of rough circumstances. But for a princess?" He shook his head.

"I want to know useful things!"

"What is useful in your world and what is

useful in mine are two very different things," he said almost gently.

Rebelliously she attacked the mango with her knife. Ten minutes later as she looked at the sliver of fruit in front of her, what was left of her mango, she realized he was probably right. Domestication at this late date was probably hopeless. She felt sticky to the elbow, and had managed to get juice in her eye. The mango was mangled beyond recognition.

She cast him a look. Ronan was taking golden-brown biscuits off a griddle above the stove. The scent of them made her mouth water.

"Here," she said, handing him the remnants of her mango. He took it wordlessly, his face a careful blank, and added it to the plate of fruit he had prepared.

She thought they'd take the food inside to the dining table, but he motioned her over to a little stone bench, set the plate down between them, lifted his face to the morning sun as he picked up a piece of fruit.

She followed his example and picked up a slice of fruit and a biscuit with her fingers.

Shoshauna had dined on the finest foods in the world. She had eaten at the fanciest tables of B'Ranasha, using the most exquisite china and cutlery. But she felt as if she had never tasted food this fine or enjoyed flavor so much.

She decided she loved everything, absolutely everything, about being an ordinary girl. And she hadn't given up on herself in the domestic department yet, either!

CHAPTER FOUR

AFTER a few minutes Shoshauna couldn't help but notice that her pleasure in the simplicity of the breakfast feast seemed to be entirely one-sided.

Ronan, while obviously enjoying the sunshine and eating with male appetite, seemed pensive, turned in on himself, as anxious not to connect with her as she *was* to connect with him.

"Are you enjoying breakfast?" she asked, craving conversation, curious about this man who had become her protector.

He nodded curtly.

She realized she was going to have to be more direct! "Tell me about yourself," she invited.

He shot her a look, looked away. "There's nothing to tell. I'm a soldier. That means my life is ninety-nine percent pure unadulterated boredom."

She supposed you didn't learn to make a bed like that if you led a life of continuous excitement, but she knew he was fudging the truth. She could tell, from the way he carried himself, from the calm with which he had handled things yesterday that he dealt with danger as comfortably as most men dealt with the reading of the morning paper.

"And one percent what?" she asked when it became apparent he was going to add nothing voluntarily.

"All hell breaking loose."

"Oh!" she said genuinely intrigued. "All hell breaking loose! That sounds exciting."

"I wish you wouldn't say that word," he said, ignoring her implied invitation to share some of his most exciting experiences with her.

"Hell, hell, hell, hell, hell," she said, and found it very liberating both to say the word and to defy him. Her society prized meekness in women, but she had made the discovery she was not eager to be anyone's prize!

He shot her a stern look. She smiled back. He wasn't her father! He didn't look more than a few years older than she was. He couldn't tell her how to behave!

He sighed, resigned, she hoped, to the fact he was not going to control her. She'd been controlled quite enough. This was her week to do whatever she wanted, including say *hell* to her heart's content.

"What's the most exciting thing that ever happened to you?" she pressed, when he actually shut his eyes, lifted his chin a bit higher to the sun, took a bite of biscuit, apparently intent on pretending he was dining alone and ignoring her questions.

He thought about it for a minute, but his reluctance to engage in this conversation was palpable. Finally he said, without even opening his eyes, "I ran into a grizzly bear while in Canada on a mountain survival exercise."

"Really?" she breathed. "What happened?" It

was better than she could have hoped. Better than a movie! She waited for him to tell her what she could picture so vividly—Ronan wrestling the primitive animal to the ground with his bare hands...

"It ran one way and I ran the other."

She frowned, sharply disappointed at his lack of heroics. "That doesn't sound very exciting!"

"I guess you had to be there."

"I think I would like to go to the mountains in Canada." Yes, even with bears, or maybe because of bears, it sounded like an adventure she'd enjoy very much. "Are the mountains beautiful? Is there snow?"

"Yes, to both."

"What's snow like?" she asked wistfully.

"Cold."

"No, what does it *feel* like." Again, he was trying to disengage, but he was the only person she'd ever met who had experienced snow, and she *had* to know.

"It's different all the time," he said, giving in

a little, as if he sensed her needing to know. "If it's very cold the snow is light and powdery, like frozen dust. If it's warmer it's heavy and wet and sticks together. You can build things with it when it's like that."

"Like a snowman?"

"Yeah, I suppose. I built a snow cave out of it."

"Which kind is better for sledding?"

"The cold, dry kind. What do you know about that?"

"Nothing. I've seen it on television. I've always had a secret desire to try it, a secret desire to see different things than here, more beautiful."

"I don't know if there's anything more beautiful than this," he said. "It's a different kind of beauty. More rugged. The landscape there is powerful rather than gentle. It reminds a person of how small they are and how big nature is." He suddenly seemed to think he was talking too much. "I'm sure your husband will take you there if you want to go," he said abruptly.

It was her turn to glare at him. She didn't want

to be reminded, at this moment, that her life was soon going to involve a husband.

"I'm fairly certain Prince Mahail," she said, "is about as interested in tobogganing in snow as he is in training a water buffalo to tap dance."

"He doesn't like traveling? Trying new things?" He did open his eyes then, lower his chin. He was regarding her now with way too much interest.

She felt a sensation in her stomach like panic. "I don't know what he likes," she said, her voice strangled. She felt suddenly like crying, looked down at her plate and blinked back the tears.

Her life had come within seconds of being linked forever to a man who was a stranger to her. And despite the fact the heavens had taken pity on her and granted her a reprieve, there was no guarantee that linking would not still happen.

"Hey," Ronan said, "hey, don't cry."

After all the events of yesterday, including being shot at, this was the first time she'd heard even the smallest hint of panic in that calm voice!

"I'm not crying," she said. But she was. She scrubbed furiously at the tear that worked its way down her cheek. She didn't want Ronan to be looking at her like that because he felt sorry for her!

She reminded herself she was supposed to be finding out about Ronan, not the other way around!

"What made you want to be a soldier?" she asked, trying desperately for an even tone of voice, to change the subject, to not waste one precious second contemplating all the adventures she was not going to have once she was married to Mahail.

Something flickered in his eyes. Sympathy? Compassion? Whatever it was, he opened up to her just the tiniest little bit.

"I had a lousy home life as a kid. I wanted routine. Stability. Rules. I found what I was looking for." He regarded her intently, hesitated and then said softly, "And you will, too. Trust me."

He would be such an easy man to trust, to believe that he had answers.

"Isn't it a hard life you've chosen?" she asked him, even though what she really wanted to say was *how? How will I ever find what I'm looking for? I don't even know where to look!*

He shrugged, tilted his chin back toward the sun. "Our unit's unofficial motto is Go Hard or Go Home. Some would see it as hard. I see it as challenging."

Was there any subtle way to ask what she most wanted to ask, besides *How will I ever find what I'm looking for?* It was inappropriate to ask him, and too soon. But still, she was not going to find herself alone on a deserted island with an extremely handsome man ever again.

She had to know. She had to know if he was available. Even though she herself, of course, was not. Not even close.

"Do you have a girlfriend?" She hoped she wasn't blushing.

He opened his eyes, shot her a look, closed them again. "No."

"Why not?"

His openness came to an abrupt end. That firm line appeared again around his mouth. "What is this? Twenty questions at the high school cafeteria?"

"What's a high school caff-a-ter-ee-a?"

"Never mind. I don't have a girlfriend because my lifestyle doesn't lend itself to having a girlfriend."

"Why?"

He sighed, but she was not going to be discouraged. Her option was to spend the week talking to him or talking to herself. At the moment she felt her survival depended on focusing on his life, rather than her own.

Maybe her desperation was apparent because he caved slightly. "I travel a lot. I can be called away from home for months at a time. I dismantle the odd bomb. I jump from airplanes."

"Meeting the grizzly bear wasn't the most exciting thing that ever happened to you!" she accused.

"Well, it was the most exciting thing that I'm

allowed to talk about. Most of what I do is highly classified."

"And dangerous."

He shrugged. "Dangerous enough that it doesn't seem fair to have a girlfriend or a family."

"I'm not sure," she said, thoughtfully, "what is unfair about being yourself?"

He looked at her curiously and she explained what she meant. "The best thing is to be passionate about life. That's what makes people really seem alive, whole, isn't it? If they aren't afraid to live the way they want to live and to live fully? That's what a girlfriend should want for you. For a life that makes you whole. And happy. Even if it is dangerous."

She was a little embarrassed that she, who had never had a boyfriend, felt so certain about what qualifications his girlfriend should have. And she was sadly aware that passion, the ability to be alive and whole, were the very qualities she herself had lost somewhere a long the way.

As if to underscore how much she had lost or

never discovered, he asked her, suddenly deciding to have a conversation after all, "So, what's the most exciting thing you've ever done?"

Been shot at. Cut my hair. Ridden a motorcycle.

All the most exciting events of her life had happened yesterday! It seemed way too pathetic to admit that, though it increased her sense of urgency, this was her week to live.

"I'm afraid that's classified," she said, and was rewarded when he smiled, ever so slightly, but spoiled the effect entirely by chucking her under her chin as if she was a precocious child, gathered their plates and stood up.

Shoshauna realized, that panicky sensation suddenly back, that she had to squeeze as much into the next week as she possibly could. "I'm putting on my bathing suit now and going swimming. Are you coming?"

He looked pained. "No. I'll look after the dishes."

"We can do the dishes later. Together. You can show me how."

He said another nice word under his breath.

She repeated it, and when he gave her *that* look, the stern, forbidding, don't-mess-with-me look, she said it again!

When he closed his eyes and took a deep breath, a man marshaling his every resource, she knew beyond a shadow of a doubt that he was dreading this week every bit as much as she was looking forward to it.

"How about if we do the dishes now?" he said. "In this climate I don't think you want to leave things out to attract bugs. And then," he added, resigned, "if you really want, I'll show you how to make biscuits."

She eyed him suspiciously. He didn't look like a man who would be the least bothered by a few bugs. He'd probably eaten them on occasion! And he certainly did not look like a man who wanted to give out cooking lessons.

So that left her with one conclusion. He didn't like the water. No, that wasn't it. And then, for some reason, she remembered the look on his face when he'd put that pink bikini back on the rack in the store yesterday.

And she understood perfectly!

Ronan did not want to see her in a bikini. Which meant, as much as he didn't want to, he found her attractive.

A shiver went up and down her spine, and she felt something she had not felt for a very long time, if she had ever felt it at all.

Without knowing it, Ronan had given her a very special gift. Princess Shoshauna felt the exquisite discovery of her own power.

"I'd love to learn to make biscuits instead of going swimming," she said meekly, the perfect B'Ranasha princess. Then she smiled to herself at the relief he was unable to mask in his features. She had a secret weapon. And she would decide when and where to use it.

"Hey," Ronan snapped, "cut it out."

The princess ignored him, took another handful of soap bubbles and blew them at him.

Princess Shoshauna had developed a gift for knowing when it was okay to ignore his instructions and when it wasn't, and it troubled him that she read him so easily after four days of being together.

He had not managed to keep her out of the bathing suit, hard as he had tried. He'd taken her at her word that she wanted to learn things and had her collecting fruit and firewood. He'd taught her how to start a decent fire, showed her edible plants, a few rudimentary survival skills.

Ronan had really thought she would lose interest in all these things, but she had not. Her fingers were covered in tiny pinpricks from her attempts to handle a needle and thread, she was sporting a bruise on one of her legs from trying to climb up a coconut tree, she gathered firewood every morning with enthusiasm and without being asked. Even her bed making was improving!

He was reluctantly aware that the princess had that quality that soldiers admired more than any other. They called it "try." It was a never-say-die, never-quit determination that was worth more in many situations than other attributes like strength and smarts, though in fact the princess had both of those, too, her strength surprising, given her physical size.

Still, busy as he'd tried to keep her, he'd failed to keep her from swimming, though he'd developed his own survival technique for when she donned the lime-green handkerchief she called a bathing suit.

The bathing suit was absolutely astonishing on her. He knew as soon as he saw it that he had been wrong thinking the pink one he'd made her put back would look better, because nothing could look better.

She was pure, one-hundred-percent-female menace in that bathing suit, slenderness and curves in a head-spinning mix. Mercifully, for him, she was shy about wearing it, and got herself to the water's edge each day before dropping the towel she wrapped herself in.

His survival technique: he went way down the

beach and spearfished for dinner while she swam. He kept an eye on her, listened for sounds of distress, kept his distance.

He was quite pleased with his plan, because she was so gorgeous in a bathing suit it could steal a man's strength as surely as Delilah had stolen Sampson's by cutting off his hair.

Shoshauna blew some more bubbles at him.

"Cut it out," he warned her again.

She chuckled, unfortunately, not the least intimidated by him anymore.

It was also unfortunately charming how much fun she was having doing the dishes. She had fun doing everything, going after life as if she had been a prisoner in a cell, marveling at the smallest things.

Hard as it was to maintain complete professionalism in the face of her joie de vivre, he was glad her mood was upbeat. There had been no more emotional outbursts after that single time she had burst into tears at the very mention of her fiancé, her husband-to-be.

Ronan could handle a lot of things, up to and including a mad mamma grizzly clicking her teeth at him and rearing to her full seven-foot height on her hind legs. But he could not handle a woman in tears!

Still he found himself contemplating that one time, in quiet moments, in the evenings when he was by himself and she had tumbled into bed, exhausted and happy. How could Shoshauna not even know if her future life partner liked traveling, or if he shared her desire to touch snow, to toboggan? The princess was, obviously, marrying a stranger. And just as obviously, and very understandably, she was terrified of it.

But all that fell clearly into the none-of-his-business category. The sense that swept over him, when he saw her shinny up a tree, grinning down at him like the cheeky little monkey she was, of being protective, almost furiously so, of wanting to rescue her from her life was inappropriate. He was a soldier. She was a princess. His life involved doing things he didn't want to do, and so did hers.

But marrying someone she didn't even really know? Glancing at her now, bubbles from head to toe, it seemed like a terrible shame. She was adorable—fun, curious, bratty, sexy as all get-out—she was the kind of girl some guy could fall head over heels in love with. And she deserved to know what that felt like.

Not, he told himself sternly, *that he was in any kind of position to decide what she did or didn't deserve. That wasn't part of the mission.*

He'd never had a mission that made him feel curiously weak instead of strong, as if things were spinning out of his control. He'd come to *like* being with her, so much so that even doing dishes with her was weakness, pure and simple.

It had been bad enough when she waltzed out in shorts every morning, her legs golden and flawless, looking like they went all the way to her belly button. Which showed today, her T-shirt a touch too small. Every time she moved her arms, he saw a flash of slender tummy.

It was bad enough that when he'd glanced over

at her, hacking away at the poor defenseless mango or pricking her fingers with a needle, he felt an absurd desire to touch her hair because it had looked spiky, sticking up all over the place like tufts of grass but he was willing to bet it was soft as duck down.

It was bad enough that she was determined to have a friendship, and that even though he knew it was taboo, sympathy had made him actually engage with her instead of discouraging her.

I had a lousy home life as a kid. That was the most personal information he'd said to anyone about himself in years. He *hated* that he'd said it, even if he'd said it to try and make her realize good things could come from bad.

He hated that sharing with her that one stupid, small sentence had made him realize a loneliness resided in him that he had managed to outrun for a long, long time. He'd said he didn't have a girlfriend because of his work, but that was only a part truth. The truth was he didn't want anyone to know him so well that they could coax information out of him that made him feel vulnerable and not very strong at all.

He was a man who loved danger, who rose to the thrill of a risk. He lived by his unit's motto, Go Hard or Go Home, and he did it with enthusiasm. His life was about intensely masculine things: strength, discipline, guts, toughness.

After his mother's great love of all things frilly and froufrou, he had not just accepted his rough barracks existence, he had embraced it. He had, consciously or not, rejected the feminine, the demands of being around the female of the species. He had no desire to be kind, polite, gentle or accommodating.

But in revealing that one small vulnerability to Shoshauna, he recognized he had never taken the greatest risk of all.

Part of the reason he was a soldier—or maybe most of the reason—was he could keep his heart in armor. He'd been building that armor, piece by meticulous piece, since the death of his dad. But when he'd asked her, that first day together,

"Who knows what love is?" he'd had a flash of memory, a realization that a place in him thought it knew exactly what love was.

There was a part of him that he most wanted to deny, that he had been very successfully denying until a few short days ago, but now it nibbled around the edges of his mind. Ronan secretly hoped there was a place a man could lay his armor down, a place he could be soft, a place where there was room to love another.

Shoshauna, without half trying, was bringing his secrets to the surface. She was way too curious and way too engaging. Luckily for him, he had developed that gift of men who did dangerous and shadowy work. He was taciturn, wary of any interest in him.

In his experience, civilians thought they wanted to know, thought a life of danger was like adventure movies, but it wasn't and they didn't.

But Shoshauna's desire to know seemed genuine, and even though she had led the most sheltered of lives, he had a feeling she could handle who he really was. More than handle it—embrace it.

But these were the most dangerous thoughts—the thoughts that jeopardized his mission, his sense of professionalism and his sense of himself.

But what had his choices been? To totally ignore her for the week? Set up a tent out back here? Pretend she didn't exist?

He was no expert on women, but he knew they liked to talk. It was in his own best interests to keep the princess moderately happy with their stay here. Hell, part of him, an unfortunately large part, *wanted* to make her happy before he returned her to a fate that he would not have wished on anyone.

Marriage seemed like a hard enough proposition without marrying someone you didn't know. Ask his mother. She'd made it her hobby to marry people she didn't really know.

A renegade thought blasted through his mind: if he was Shoshauna's prince, he'd take her to that mountaintop just because she wanted to go, just to see the delight in her face when she looked down over those sweeping valleys, to see her inhale the crispness of the air. He'd build snowmen with her and race toboggans down breathtakingly steep slopes just to hear the sound of her laughter.

If he was her prince? Cripes, he was getting in bigger trouble by the minute.

There had been mistakes made over the past few days. One of them had been asking her about the most exciting thing in her life. Because it had been so pathetically evident it had probably been that motorcycle ride and all of *this*.

From the few words she'd said about passion he'd known instantly that she regretted the directions of her own life, *yearned* for more. And he'd been taken by her wisdom, too, when he'd told her that the dangerous parts of his job kept him from a relationship.

Was there really a woman out there who understood that caring about someone meant encouraging her partner to pursue what made him whole and alive? Not in his experience there wasn't! Beginning with his mother, it was always about how *she* felt, what *she* needed to feel safe, secure, loved. Not that it had ever worked for her, that strangling kind of love that wanted to control and own.

The last thing he wanted to be thinking about was his mother! Even the bathing suit would be better than that. He was aware the thought of his mother had appeared because he had opened the door a crack when he admitted he had a lousy childhood. That was the whole problem with admissions like that.

He was here, on this island, with the princess, to do a simple job. To protect her. And that meant he did not—thank God—have the luxury of looking at himself right now.

Still, he knew he had to be very, very careful because he was treading a fine line. He'd already felt the uncomfortable wriggle of emotion for her. He didn't want to be rude, but he had to make it very clear, to himself and to her, this was his job. He wasn't on vacation, he wasn't supposed to be having fun.

He couldn't even allow himself to think the thoughts of a normal, healthy man when he saw her in that bathing suit every day.

But now he was wondering if he'd overrated that danger and underrated this one. Because in the bathing suit she was sexy. Untouchable and sexy, like a runway model or a film actress. He could watch her from a safe distance, up the beach somewhere, sunglasses covering his eyes so she would never read his expression.

With soap bubbles all over her from washing dishes, she was still sexy. But cute, too. He was not quite sure how she had managed to get soap bubbles all over the long length of her naked legs, but she had.

She put bubbles on her face, a bubble beard and moustache. "Look!"

"How old are you?" he asked, putting duty first, pretending pure irritation when in fact her enjoyment of very small things was increasingly enchanting.

"Twenty-one."

"Well, quit acting like you're six," he said.

Then he felt bad, because she looked so crest-fallen. *Boundaries,* yes, but he was not going to do that again: try to erect them by hurting her feelings. He'd crossed the fine line between being rude and erecting professional barriers. Ronan simply expected himself to be a better man than that.

Against his better judgment, but by way of apology, he scooped up a handful of suds and tossed them at her. She tossed some back. A few minutes later they were both drenched in suds and laughing.

Great. The barriers were down almost completely, when he had vowed to get them back up—when he knew her survival depended on it. And perhaps his own, too.

Still, despite the fact he knew he was dancing with the kind of danger that put meeting a grizzly bear to shame, it occurred to him, probably because of the seriousness of most of his work, he'd forgotten how to be young.

He was only twenty-seven, but he'd done work that had aged him beyond that, stolen his laughter. The kind of dark, gallows humor he shared with his comrades didn't count.

Even when the guys played together, they played rough, body-bruising sports, the harder hitting the better. He had come to respect strength and guts, and his world was now almost exclusively about those things. There was no room in it for softness, not physical, certainly not emotional.

His work often required him to be mature way beyond his years, required him to shoulder responsibility that would have crippled any but the strongest of men. Life was so often serious, decisions so often involved life and death, that he had forgotten how to be playful, had forgotten how good it could feel to laugh like this.

The rewards of his kind of work were many: he felt a deep sense of honor; he felt as if he made a real difference in a troubled world; he was proud of his commitment to be of service to his fellow man; the bonds he had with his brothers in arms were stronger than steel. Ronan had never questioned the price he paid to do the work before, and he absolutely knew now was not the time to start!

Sharing a deserted island with a gorgeous princess who was eager to try on her new bikini, was absolutely the wrong time to decide to re-discover those things!

But just being around her made him so aware of *softness,* filled him with a treacherous yearning. The full meltdown could probably start with something as simple as wanting to touch her hair.

"Okay," he said, serious, trying to be very serious, something light still lingering in his heart, "you want to learn how to make my secret biscuit recipe?"

Ronan had done many different survival schools. All the members of Excalibur prided themselves in their ability to produce really good food from limited ingredients, to use what they could find around them. He was actually more comfortable cooking over a fire than he was using an oven.

An hour later with flour now deeply stuck on her damp skin, she pulled her biscuit attempt from the wood-fired oven.

Ronan tried to keep a straight face. Every biscuit was a different size. Some were burned and some were raw.

"Try one," she insisted.

Since he'd already hurt her feelings once today and decided that wasn't the way to keep his professional distance, he sucked it up and took one of the better-looking biscuits.

He took a big bite. "Hey," he lied, "not bad for a first try."

She helped herself to one, wrinkled her nose, set it down. "I'll try again tomorrow."

He hoped she wouldn't. He hoped she'd tire soon of the novelty of working together, because it was fun, way more fun than he wanted to have with her.

"Let's go swimming now," she said. "Could you come with me today? I thought I saw a shark yesterday."

Was that pure devilment dancing in the turquoise of those eyes? Of course it was. She'd figured out he didn't want to swim with her, figured out her softness was piercing his armor in ways no bullet ever had. She'd figured out how badly he didn't want to be anywhere near her when she was in that bathing suit.

In other words, she had figured out his weakness.

He could not let her see that. One thing he'd learned as a soldier was you never ran away from the thing that scared you the most. Never. You ran straight toward it.

"Sure," he said, with a careless shrug. "Let's go."

He said it with the bravado of a man who had just been assigned to dismantle a bomb and didn't want a single soul to know how scared he was.

But when he looked into her eyes, dancing with absolute mischief, he was pretty sure he had not pulled it off.

She was not going to be fooled by him, and it was a little disconcerting to feel she could see through him so completely when he had become such an expert at hiding every weakness he ever felt.

CHAPTER FIVE

SHOSHAUNA stared at herself in the mirror in her bedroom and gulped. The bathing suit was really quite revealing. It hadn't seemed to matter so much when Ronan was way down the shoreline, spearfishing, picking up driftwood, but today he was going to swim with her! Finally.

She could almost hear her mother reacting to her attire. "Common." Her father would be none to pleased with this outfit, either, especially since she was in the company of a man, completely unchaperoned.

But wasn't that the whole problem with her life? She had been far to anxious to please others and not nearly anxious enough to please herself. She had always dreamed of being bold, of being the adventurer, but in the end she had always backed away.

She remembered the exhilarating sense of power she had felt when she realized Ronan didn't want to see this bathing suit, when she'd realized, despite all his determination not to, he found her attractive. Suddenly she wanted to feel that power again. She was so aware of the clock ticking. They had been here four days. There was three left, and then it would be over.

Suddenly nothing could have kept her from the sea, and Ronan.

At the last minute, though, as always, she wrapped a huge bath towel around herself before she stepped out of the house.

Ronan waited outside the door, glanced at her, his expression deadpan, but she was sure she saw a glint of amusement in his eyes, as if he *knew* she was really too shy to wear that bikini with confidence, with delight in her own power when there was a man in such close quarters.

"Look what I found under the porch," he said.

Two sets of snorkels and fins! No one could look sexy or feel powerful in a snorkel and fins! Still, she had not snorkeled since the last time she had been here, and she remembered the experience with wonder.

"Was the surfboard there?"

"Yeah, an old longboard. You want me to grab it? You could paddle around on it."

"No, thank you," she said. Paddle around on it, as if she was a little kid at the wading pool. She wanted to surf on it—to capture the power of the sea—or nothing at all. Just to prove to him she was not a little kid, *at all,* she yanked the towel away.

He dropped his sunglasses down over his eyes rapidly, took a sudden interest in the two sets of snorkels and fins, but she could see his Adam's apple jerk each time he swallowed.

She marched down the sand to the surf, trying to pretend she was confident as could be but entirely aware she was nearly naked and in way over her head without even touching the water. She plunged into the sea as quickly as she could.

Once covered by the blanket of the ocean, she turned back, pretending complete confidence.

"The water is wonderful," she called. "Come in." It was true, the water was wonderful, warm, a delight she had been discovering all week was even better against almost-naked skin.

Suddenly she was glad she'd found the courage to wear the bikini, glad she'd left the towel behind, glad she was experiencing how sensuous it was to be in the water with hardly anything between it and her, not even fabric. Her new haircut was perfect for swimming, too! Not heavy with wetness, it dried almost instantly in the sun.

She looked again at the beach. Ronan was watching her, arms folded over his chest, like a lifeguard at the kiddy park.

She was going to get that kiddy-park look off his face if it killed her!

"Come in," she called again, and then pressed the button she somehow knew, by instinct, he could not stand to have pressed. "Unless you're scared."

Not of the water, either, but of her. She felt a

little swell of that feeling, *power,* delicious, seductive, pure feminine power. She had been holding off with it, waiting, uncertain, but now the time felt right.

She watched as Ronan dropped the snorkeling gear in the sand, pulled his shirt over his head. She felt her mouth go dry. This was how she had hoped he would react to her. A nameless yearning engulfed her as she stared at the utter magnificence of his build.

He was pure and utter male perfection. Every fluid inch of him was about masculine strength, a body honed to the perfection of a hard fighting tool.

Shoshauna had thought she would feel like the powerful one if they swam together, but now she could see the power was in the chemistry itself, not in her, not in him.

There was a universal force that called when a certain woman looked at a certain man, when a certain man looked at a certain woman. It pulled them together, an ancient law of attraction, metal

to magnet, a law irresistible, as integral as gravity
to the earth.

Shoshauna became aware that the "power" she
had so wanted to experiment with, to play with,
was out of her control. She felt a kind of helpless
thrill, like a child who had played with matches
and was now having to deal with a renegade
spark that had flared to flame.

Impossible to put this particular fire out. Ronan
was all sleek muscle and hard lines, not an ounce
of superfluous fat or flesh on his powerful male
body. His chest was deep, his stomach flat, ridged
with ab muscles, his shoulders impossibly broad.
His legs were long, rippling with muscle.

He dove cleanly into the water, cutting it with
his body. Two powerful strokes carried him to
her, another beyond her. She watched, mesmer-
ized, as his strong crawl carried him effortlessly
out into the bay. He stopped twenty or thirty
yards from her, trod water, shook diamond
droplets of the sea from his hair.

Watching him, she realized what she had been

doing could not even really be called swimming. She was paddling. No wonder he treated her as if she belonged in the kiddy pool! Bathing suit aside, in the water she was an elephant trying to keep pace with a cheetah!

Ronan flipped over on his back, spread his arms like a star and floated. It looked so comfortable, so relaxing that she tried it and nearly drowned. She came up sputtering for air.

"Are you okay?"

And what if she wasn't? Would he swim over here, gather her in his arms, maybe give her mouth-to-mouth resuscitation?

"I'm fine," she squeaked.

He did swim back over, but did not come too close. "You're about as deep as you should go," he told her. "I've noticed over the past few days you are not a very strong swimmer."

"In my mother's mind swimming in the ocean was an activity for the sons and daughters of fishermen."

"It seems a shame to live in a place like this, surrounded by water and not know how to swim. It seems foolish to me, unnecessarily risky, because with this much water you're eventually going to have an encounter with it." Hastily he added, "Not that I'm calling your mother foolish."

"Plus, she has this thing about showing skin." And that was with a *regular* bathing suit.

Ronan eyed her. "I take it she wouldn't approve of the bathing suit."

He *had* noticed.

"She'd have a heart attack," Shoshauna admitted.

"It's having just about the same effect on me," he said with a rueful grin, taking all her power away by admitting he'd noticed, a man incapable of pretense, *real,* just as she'd known he was.

"That's why your mom doesn't want you wearing stuff like that. Men are evil creatures, given to drawing conclusions from visual clues that aren't necessarily correct."

Back to the kiddy pool! He was going to turn this into a lecture. But he didn't. He left it at that, yet she felt a little chastened anyway.

As if he sensed that, he quickly changed the subject. "So, I've got you out here in the water. Want to—"

Was she actually hoping he was going to propose something a little evil?

"Want to learn how to swim a little better?"

She nodded, both relieved and annoyed by his ability to treat her like a kid, his charge, nothing more.

"You won't be ready to enter the Olympics after one lesson, but if you fall out of a boat, you'll be able to survive."

It had probably been foolish to suggest teaching Shoshauna to swim. But the fact of the matter was she lived on an island. She was around water all the time. It seemed an unbelievable oversight to him that her education had not included swimming lessons.

On the other hand, what did he know about what skills a princess needed? Still, he felt he could leave here a better man knowing that if she did fall off a boat, she could tread water until she was rescued.

Probably he was kidding himself that he was teaching her something important. If a princess fell overboard, surely ten underlings jumped in the water after her.

But somehow it was increasingly important to him that she know how to save herself. And maybe not just if she fell off a boat. All these things he had been teaching her this week were skills that made no sense for a princess.

But for a woman coming into herself, learning the power of self-reliance seemed vital. It felt important that if he gave her nothing else, he gave her a taste of that: what her potential was, what she was capable of doing and learning if she set her mind to it.

Because Ronan was Australian and had grown up around beaches and heavy surf, he had quite often been chosen to instruct other members of Excalibur in survival swimming.

Thankfully, he could teach just about anybody to swim without ever laying a hand on them.

She was a surprisingly eager student, more willing to try things in the water than many a seasoned soldier. Like the things she had been doing on land, he soon realized she had no fear, and she learned very quickly. By the end of a half hour, she could tread water for a few minutes, had the beginnings of a not bad front crawl and could do exactly two strokes of a backstroke before she sank and came up sputtering.

And then disaster struck, the kind, from teaching soldiers, he was totally unprepared for.

She was treading water, when her mouth formed a startled little *O*. She forgot to sweep the water, wrapped her arms around herself and promptly sank.

His mind screamed *shark* even though he had evaluated the risks of swimming in the bay and decided they were minimal.

When she didn't bob right back to the surface, he was at her in a second, dove, wrapped his arm around her waist, dragged her up. No sign of a shark, though her arms were still tightly wrapped around her chest.

Details. Part of him was trying to register what was wrong, when she sputtered something incomprehensible and her face turned bright, bright red.

"My top," she sputtered.

For a second he didn't comprehend what she was saying, and when he did he was pretty sure the heart attack he'd teased her about earlier was going to happen for real. He had his arms around a nearly naked princess.

He let go of her so fast she started to sink again, unwilling to unwrap her arms from around her naked bosom.

Somehow her flimsy top had gone missing!

"Swim in to where you can stand up," he ordered her sharply.

He knew exactly what tone to use on a frightened soldier to ensure instant obedience, and it worked on her. She headed for shore, doing a clumsy one-armed crawl—her other arm still firmly clamped over her chest—that he might have found funny if it was anyone but her. As soon as he made sure she was standing up on the ocean bottom, he looked around.

The missing article was floating several yards away. He swam over and grabbed it, knew it was the wrong time to think how delicate it felt, how fragile in his big, rough hands, what a flimsy piece of material to be given so much responsibility.

He came up behind her. She was standing up to her shoulder blades in water and still had a tight wrap on herself, but there was no hiding the naked line of her back, the absolute feminine perfection of her.

"I'll look away," he said, trying to make her feel as if it was no big deal. "You put it back on."

Within minutes she had the bathing suit back on, but she wouldn't look at him. And he was finding it very difficult to look at her.

Wordlessly she left the water, spread out her towel and lay down on her stomach. She still wouldn't even look at him and he figured maybe that was a good thing. He put on the snorkeling gear and headed back out into the bay.

He began to see school after school of butterfly fish, many that he recognized as the same as he would see in the reefs off Australia: the distinctive yellow, white and black stripes of the threadfin, the black splash of color that identified the teardrop.

Suddenly, Ronan didn't want her to stay embarrassed all day, just so that he could be protected from his own vulnerability around her. He didn't want her to miss the enchantment of the reef fish.

Her embarrassment over the incident was a good reminder to him that she had grown up very sheltered. She had sensed the bikini would get his attention, but she hadn't known what to do with it when she succeeded.

In his world, girls were fast and flirty and knew exactly what to do with male attention. Her innocence in a bold world made him want to share the snorkeling experience with her even more.

They would focus on the fish, the snorkeling, not each other.

"Shoshauna! Put on a snorkel and fins. You have to see this."

He realized he'd called her by her first name, as if they were friends, as if it was *okay* for them to snorkel together, to share these moments.

Too late to back out, though. She joined him in the water, but not before tugging on her bathing suit strings about a hundred times to make sure they were secure.

And then she was beside him, and the magic happened. They swam into a world of such beauty it was almost incomprehensible. Fish in psychedelic colors that ranged from brilliant orange to electric blue swam around them. They saw every variety of damselfish, puffer fish, triggerfish, surgeonfish.

He tapped her shoulder. "Watch those ones," he said, pointing at an orange band. "It's a type of surgeonfish, they're called that because their spines are scalpel sharp."

Her wonder was palpable when a Moorish idol investigated her with at least as much interest as she was giving it! A school of the normally shy neon-green and blue palenose parrot fishes swam around her as if she was part of the sea.

He was not sure when he lost interest in the fish and focused instead on her reaction to them. Ronan was not sure he had seen anything as lovely as the awed expression on her face when a bluestripe snapper kissed her hand.

He was breaking all the rules. And somehow it seemed worth it. And somehow he didn't care. Time evaporated, and he was stunned when he saw the sun going down in the sky.

They went in to shore, dried the saltwater off with towels. He saw she was looking at him with a look that was both innocent and hungry.

"I'm going to cook dinner," he said gruffly. Suddenly breaking the rules didn't seem as great, it didn't seem worth it, and he did care.

He cared because he felt something, and he knew it was huge. He felt the desire to *know* someone. He *wanted* to know her better. He *wanted* things he had never wanted and that, in this case, he knew he could never have.

These four days together had created an illusion that they were just two normal people caught up together. These days had allowed him to see her as real, as few people had ever seen her. These days had allowed him to see her, and he had liked what he had seen. It was natural to want to know more, to explore where this affinity he felt for her could go.

But the island was a fantasy, one so strong it had diluted reality, made him forget reality.

He was a soldier. She was a princess. Their worlds were a zillion miles apart. She was promised to someone else.

With those facts foremost in his mind, he cooked dinner, refusing her offer to help, and he was brusque with her when she asked him if he knew the name of a bright-yellow snout-nosed fish they had seen. She took the hint and they ate in blessed silence. Why did he miss being peppered with her questions? Did she, too, realize that a dangerous shift had happened between them?

Still, getting ready for bed, he was congratulating himself on what a fine job he'd done on reerecting the barriers, when he heard an unmistakable whimper from her room.

Surely she wasn't that embarrassed over her brief nude scene?

He knew he had to ignore her, but then she cried out again, the sound muffled, as if she had a blanket stuffed in her mouth. It was the sound being stifled that made him bolt from his room, and barge through her door.

She was alone, in bed. No enemy had crept up on him while he'd been busy playing reef guide instead of doing his job.

"What's the matter?" He squinted at her through the darkness.

The sheet was pulled up around her, right to her chin.

"I hurt so bad."

"What do you mean?"

He lit the hurricane lamp that had been left on a chair just inside her door, moved to the side of her bed and gazed down at her. She reluctantly pulled the sheet down just enough to show him her shoulders. That's why she had been quiet at dinner.

Not embarrassed, not taking the hint that he didn't want to talk to her, but in pain. Even in the light of the lantern he could clearly see she was badly sunburned. Cursing himself silently, he wondered how close she had come to heat exhaustion.

White lines where her bikini straps had been were in sharp contrast to her skin.

Because her skin tones were so golden it had never occurred to him she might burn. It had not seemed scorchingly hot out today. On the other hand he should have known breezes coming off the water could make it seem cooler than it was. It had never occurred to him that someone who lived in this island paradise might not avail themselves of the outdoors.

He remembered, too late, what she had said about her mother. "Has your skin ever seen the sun before?" he asked her.

She shook her head, contrite. "Not for a long time. I was allowed to come here until I was about thirteen, but then my mother thought I was getting to be too much of a tomboy. She thought skin darkened by the sun was—"

"Let me guess," he said dryly. "Common."

He was rewarded with a weak smile from her. Selfish bastard that he was he thought, *At least I'm not going to have to see her in a bikini again for the three days we have left here on the island.*

But there was another test he had to pass right now. He was going to have to administer first aid to her burns. She'd exposed her back to the sun while they snorkeled. The water beading on it had drawn the sun like a magnet. Though her shoulders were very red looking, most of that burn was going to be on her back where she couldn't reach it herself.

Having grown up in Australia, he was cautious of the sun, but his skin was also more acclimatized to sun than that of most of the people he worked with. He did not have fair coloring, his skin seemed to like the sun.

But many times after long training days in the sun, especially desert training, soldiers were hurting. Ronan had learned lots of ways to ease the sting with readily available ingredients: either vinegar or baking soda added to bath water could bring relief. Unfortunately, just as when he was in the field, they didn't have a bath here.

What they did have was aspirin, he had seen that in a cabinet in the outdoor kitchen, and powdered milk, an ingredient he'd used before to field dress a sunburn.

He knew, though, there was going to be a big difference between placing soothing dressings cooled with freshly made milk onto her back, and slapping it onto a fellow soldier's.

All day he'd struggled to at least keep the

physical barriers between them up, since the emotional ones seemed to be falling faster than he could reerect them. When she'd lost the top, and he'd wrapped his arms around her to pull her back to the water's surface, he'd known he had to avoid going to that place again at all costs, skin against skin.

But here he was at that place again. It almost felt as if the universe was conspiring against him.

But she was his charge. He had no choice. He felt guilty that she'd gotten burned on his watch in the first place. It was proof, really, he could not be trusted with softer things, more tender things, things that required a gentle touch.

It was proof, too, that he was preoccupied, missing the details that he had always been so good at catching.

"Come on out to the kitchen," he said gruffly. "I'll put something on that that will make it feel better."

"I can't get dressed," she told him, and blushed. "My skin feels like its shrinking. I don't think I can move my arms. I don't want to put anything on that touches my skin."

Oh well, just run out there naked then.

He yanked the sheet out from the bottom of the bed and tucked it around her right up to her chin. "Come on."

She wobbled out behind him to the kitchen, the sheet draped clumsily over her, him uncomfortably and acutely aware that underneath it she was probably as naked as the day she was born. The outfit was somehow as dangerous—maybe more so—than the bikini had been.

And the night was dangerous—the stars like jewels in the night sky, the flowers releasing their perfume with a gentle and seductive vengeance.

"Sit," he said, swinging a chair out for her. He took a deep breath, prayed for strength and then did what had to be done. He lifted the sheet away from her back, forced himself to be clinical.

Her back looked so tender with burn that he forgot how awkward this situation was. The marks where her bikini strings had been tied up dissected it, at her neck and midback, white lines in stark contrast to the rest of her. Her skin was glowing bright red on top of her copper tones.

"I hate to be the bearer of bad news," he said, his sympathy genuine, his guilt acute even though he knew how hard it was to spot a burn as it was happening in the full sunlight, "but in the next few days your skin is going to be peeling. It may even blister."

"Really?" she asked.

She couldn't possibly sound, well, *pleased,* rather than distressed.

He had to make it a bit clearer. "Um, you could probably be lizard lady at the sideshow for a week or two."

"Really?" she said, again.

No doubt about it. Definitely pleased.

"Is there some reason that would make you happy?" he asked.

"Between my new hair and lizard lady, Prince Mahail will probably call off the wedding. Indefinitely."

Now there was no mistaking the pleasure in her voice.

Don't ask, Ronan. "Is he really that superficial?"

"He chose me for my hair!"

Well, he'd asked. Now he had to deal with the rush of indignation he felt. A man chose a wife for her *hair?*

It was primitive and tyrannical. It was not what she deserved. Wasn't he in the business of protecting democracy? Of protecting people's freedoms and right to choose? If she was being forced into this, then what? Cause an international incident by imposing his values on B'Ranasha, by rescuing the princess from her fate?

"Are you being forced to marry him?" he asked.

"Not exactly."

"What does that mean?"

"Nobody forced me to say yes, but there was enormous pressure, the weight of everybody's expectations."

He turned from her quickly to stave off the impulse to shake her. Here he'd been thinking he had to rescue her when the aggravating truth was she had not, as far as he could see, made a single move to rescue herself. She seemed to just be blindly trusting *something* was going to happen to get her out of her marriage. And much as he hated to admit it, so far that had worked not too badly for her.

But her luck was going to run out, and for a take-charge kind of guy, relying on luck to determine fate was about the worst possible policy.

Rather than share that with her, or allow her to see the fury he felt with her, Ronan busied himself mixing a solution of powdered milk and water in a big bowl. He tore several clean tea towels into rags and submerged them in the mixture.

Then, his unwanted surge of emotion under control, a gladiator who had no choice but the ring, he turned back to her, lifted the sheet off her back.

"Hold that up for me."

He laid the first of the milk-soaked rags flat on her naked back, smoothed it on with his hands. She seemed unbelievably delicate. Her skin was hot beneath the dressing. And, for now anyway, before the inevitable peeling, it felt incredibly smooth, flawless beneath his fingertips. He didn't know of any other way to bring her comfort, but touching her like this was intimate enough to make him feel faintly crazy, a purely primitive longing welling up within him.

He thought she might flinch, but instead she gave a little moan of pleasure and relief as the first cool, milk-soaked dressing adhered to her back, a sound that could have easily been made in another context.

"Oh," she breathed. "That feels so good. I don't think I've ever felt anything that good."

His wicked male mind wondered just how innocent that made her. Plenty innocent. And it was his job to keep it that way.

He thought about a man he had never seen, whom he knew nothing about, becoming her husband, being trusted with her delicacy, and he felt another unwanted stab of strong emotion.

Not jealousy, he told himself, God forbid, not

jealousy, just an extension of his job. Protectiveness.

But he knew it wasn't exactly a part of his job to wonder, was that man whom she had almost married, worthy of her? Would her prince be able to make her pleasure as important as his own when the time came? Would he be tender and considerate? Would he stoke the fire that burned in her eyes, or would he put it out?

Ronan, he reprimanded himself. *Stop it!* By her own admission, she was not being forced into anything. It was her problem not his.

Still, the feeling of craziness intensified, he felt a sudden primitive need to *show* her what it *should* feel like, all heat and passion, tenderness and exquisite pleasure. If she'd ever experienced what was *real* between a man and a woman she wouldn't accept a substitute, no matter how much pressure she thought she felt.

She was seriously going to pay with her life to relieve a little temporary pressure from her folks?

He gave himself a fierce mental shake. His

thinking was ludicrous, totally unacceptable, completely corrupted by emotion. He had known her less than a full week, which really meant he did not know her at all!

He was not dating her, he was protecting her. Imagining his lips on her lips was not a part of the mission.

Who would have thought he would end up having to protect the princess from himself?

"Leave those dressings on there for twenty minutes," he said, his voice absolutely flat, not revealing one little bit of his inner struggle, the madness that was threatening to envelope him. "Unfortunately in this heat the residue of the milk will start to sour if you leave it on overnight. You're going to have to rinse off in the shower before you go back to bed." He passed her some aspirin and a glass of water.

"This will take the sting out." He sounded as if he was reading from a first-aid manual. "Drink all the water, too, just in case you're a bit dehydrated. I think you'll sleep like a baby after all this."

She probably would, too, but he was wondering if he was ever going to sleep again!

Fixing her up had taken way too long, even with him trying to balance a gentle touch with his urgency to get this new form of torture over with.

"I'll head back to bed, I'll leave this lamp for you. You can peel those dressings off by yourself in twenty minutes or so. Don't forget to shower."

"All right."

"You should be okay for a few hours. If the pain comes back, starts bugging you, wake me up. We'll do it all again." He had to suck it up to even make that offer. He didn't want to touch her back again, have her naked under a sheet, the two of them alone in a place just a little too much like paradise.

No wonder Adam and Eve had gone for the apple!

"Ronan?" Her voice was husky. She touched his arm.

He froze, aware he was holding his breath, scared of what could happen next, if she asked him to stay with her. Scared of the physical attraction, scared of the thoughts he had had earlier.

"What?" He growled.

"Thank you so much."

What was he expecting? She was burned to a crisp. The last thing on her mind was, well, the thing that was on his mind. Which was her lips, soft and pliable, and how they would feel underneath his, how they would taste.

"Just doing my job."

She glanced over her shoulder at him. Her eyes met his. There was no mistaking the heat and the hunger that changed their color from turquoise to a shade of indigo. He realized it wasn't the last thing on her mind after all. That one small push from the universe and they'd be all over each other, burn or no burn. The awareness that sizzled in the air between them put that burn on her back to shame.

He sucked in a deep breath, then ducked his head, turned abruptly and walked quickly away from her.

It took more discipline to do that than to do two hundred push-ups at the whim of a aggravated sergeant, to make a bed perfectly for the thousandth time, to jump out of an airplane from twenty thousand feet in the dead of the night. Way more.

He glanced at his watch to check the date. He had to get control over this situation before it deteriorated any more.

But when he thought of her shaking droplets of water from the jagged tips of her hair, laughing, the tenderness of her back underneath the largeness of his hands, he felt a dip in the bottom of his belly.

He focused on it, but it wasn't that familiar warning, his *sideways* feeling. It was a warmth as familiar as the sun and as necessary to life.

What had happened to his warning system? Had it become dismantled? Ronan wondered if he had lost some part of himself that he *needed* in the turquoise depths of her eyes.

Isn't that what he'd learned about love from

his mother? That relationships equaled the surrender of power?

"You are not having a relationship with her," he told himself sternly, but the words were hollow, and he knew he had already crossed lines he didn't want to cross.

But tomorrow was a new day, a new battle. He was a warrior and he fully intended to recapture his lost power.

CHAPTER SIX

SHOSHAUNA took a deep breath, slid a look at Ronan. He was intense this morning, highly focused, but not on her. She could not look at him—at the dark, neat hair, his face freshly shaven, the soft gold brown of his eyes, the sheer male beauty of the way he carried himself— without feeling a shiver, remembering his hands on her back last night.

"Are you mad at me?"

"Princess?" he asked, his voice flat, as if he had no idea what she was talking about.

"Yesterday you called me Shoshauna," she said.

He said nothing; he did not look at her. He had barely spoken to her all morning. She'd gotten up and managed to get dressed, a painful process given the sunburn. Still, she had been more aware of something hammering in her heart, a desire to see him again, to be with him, than of the pain of that burn.

But Ronan had been nowhere to be found when she had come out of her bedroom. He'd left a breakfast of fresh biscuits and cut fruit for her, not outside on the bench where she had grown accustomed to sharing casual meals with him, but at the dining room table, at a place perfectly set for one.

Shoshauna had rebelled against the formality of it and taken a plate outside. As she ate she could hear the thunk of an ax biting into wood in the distance. Just as she was finishing the last of the biscuits, he dragged a tree into their kitchen clearing.

Watching him work, hauling that tree, straining against it, that *awareness* tingled through her, the same as she had felt yesterday when she had watched him strip off his shirt before swimming. She felt as if she was vibrating from it. Ronan was so one hundred percent man, all easy strength and formidable will.

Even to her inexperienced eye it looked as if he was bringing in enough wood to keep the stove fired up for about five years.

"Good morning, Ronan." Good grief, she could hear the *awareness* in her voice, a husky breathlessness.

She knew how much she had come to live for his smile when he withheld it. Instead, he'd barely said good morning, biting it out as if it hurt him to be polite. Then he was focusing on the wood he'd brought in. After using a handsaw to reduce the tree to blocks, he set a chunk on a stump chopping block, swung the ax over his head, and down into the wood.

The whole exercise of reducing the tree to firewood was a demonstration—entirely un-conscious on his part—of pure masculine strength, and she could feel her heart skip a beat every time he lifted the ax with easy, thoughtless grace. She remembered again the strength in those hands, tempered last night, and shivered.

But today his strength was not tempered at all. He certainly *seemed* angry, the wood splintering into a thousand pieces with each mighty whack of the ax blade, tension bunching his muscles, his face smooth with a total lack of expression.

He had not even asked her how her sunburn felt, and it felt terrible. Could she be bold enough to ask him to dress it again? She felt as if she was still trembling inside from the way his hands had felt pressing those soothing cloths onto her back last night. But he looked angry this morning, remote, not the same man who had been so tender last night.

"Ronan?" she pressed, even though it was obvious he didn't want to talk. "Are you angry about something?"

Actually, something in him seemed to have shifted last night when he had questioned her about her marriage. He had gone very quiet after she had admitted she wasn't being forced to marry anyone.

"No, ma'am, I'm not angry. What's to be angry about?"

"Stop it!"

He set down the ax, wiped the sweat off his forehead with a quick lift of his shirt collar, then folded his arms over his chest, looked askance at her.

"I didn't mean chopping the wood," she said, knowing he had misunderstood her deliberately.

"What did you mean then, Princess?"

"Why are you being so formal? You weren't like this yesterday."

"Yesterday," he said tightly, "was a mistake. I forgot myself, and it's not going to happen again."

"Having fun, going snorkeling was forgetting yourself?"

"Yes, ma'am."

"If you call me ma'am one more time, I'm going to throw this coconut right at your large, overweight head!"

"I think you might mean my big, fat head."

"That's exactly what I meant!"

He actually looked as though he might smile, but if he was amused he doused it quickly.

"Princess," he said, his patience elaborate and annoying, "I'm at work. I'm on the clock. I'm not here to have fun. I'm not here to teach you to swim or to identify yellow tangs for you. My job is to protect you, to keep you safe until I can get you back to your home."

"I could have been assassinated while you were out there chopping down the jungle," she said, aware her tone was growing snippy with impatience. How could he possibly not want more of what they'd had yesterday?

Not just the physical touch, though that had filled her with a hunger that felt ravenous, a tiger that needed to be fed, but the laughter, the easy camaraderie between them. It was that she found herself craving even more. How could it be that he did not want the same things?

"I think," he said dryly, "if assassins had arrived on the island, I would have heard a boat. Or a helicopter. I was only a few seconds away."

He was deliberately missing the point! "Bitten by a snake, then!"

He didn't answer, and she hated that he was treating her like a precocious child, though for some reason his attitude was making her act like one.

"Eaten by a tiger," she muttered. "Attacked by a monkey."

He sent her one irritated look, went back to the wood.

"I'm making a point! There is no danger here. None. No assassins, no snakes, no tigers, no mad monkeys. It would be perfectly fine for you to relax your vigilance."

Crash. The wood splintered. He gathered the splinters, tossed them in a pile, wouldn't look at her. "I relaxed yesterday. You got a large, over-weight sunburn because of it."

"You are not feeling responsible for that, are you?" His lack of a response was all the answer she needed. "Ronan, it wasn't your fault. It's not as if it was life threatening, anyway. A little sunburn. I can hardly feel it today." Which was a lie, but if it got rid of that look from his face— a look of cool professional detachment—it would be a lie worth telling.

He said nothing, and she knew this was about more than a sunburn.

"Are you mad because I *agreed* to get married?"

Bull's-eye. Something hard and cold in his face shook her. "That falls squarely in the none-of-my-business category."

"That's not true. We're friends. I want to talk to you about it." And suddenly she did. She felt that if she talked to Ronan, all the chaos and uncertainty inside her would subside. She felt that the terrible loneliness that had eaten at her ever since she said yes to Prince Mahail would finally go away.

She felt as if she would know what to do.

"My cat died," she blurted out. "That's why I agreed to marry him."

It felt good to say it out loud, though she could tell by the look on his face he now thought she was certifiably insane.

"But you have to understand about the cat," she said in a rush.

"No," he said, holding up his hand, a clear stop signal. "No, I don't have to understand about the cat. I don't want you telling me about your personal life. Nothing. No cat. No marriage. Not what is on or off your mother's approval list, though we both know that what isn't on it is cavorting in the ocean in a bathing suit top that is unstable with a man you barely know."

"I do know you," she protested.

"No you don't. We can't be friends," he said quietly. "Do you get that?"

She had thought they were past that, that they were already well on their way to being friends, and possibly even something more than friends. These last few days she had shared more with him than she could remember sharing with anyone. She had felt herself opening around him, like a flower opening to sunshine.

He made her discover things about herself that she hadn't known. Being around him made her feel strong and competent. And alive. It was *easy* to be herself with him. How could he say they could not be friends?

"No," she said stubbornly. "I don't get it."

"Actually," he said tersely, "it doesn't really matter if you get it or not, just as long as I get it."

She felt desperate. It was as if he was on a raft and she was on shore, and the distance between them was growing. She needed to bring him back, any way she could. "Okay, I won't tell you anything about me. Nothing."

He looked skeptical, so she rushed on, desperate. "I'll put a piece of tape over my mouth. But I can't go out in the sun today. I was hoping you'd teach me how to play chess. My mother felt chess was a very masculine game, that girls should not play it."

Even though he'd specifically told her not to mention her mother to him, she took a chance and believed she had been right to do so, because something flickered in his eyes.

He *knew* she'd be a good chess player if she got

the chance, but if he'd realized that, he doused
the thought as quickly as his smile of moments
ago. He was silent, refusing the bait.

"Do you know how to play chess?" If she could
just get him to sit down with her, spend time
with her, soon it would be easy again and fun.
She wanted to know so much about him. She
wanted him to know so much about her. They
only had a few days left! He couldn't spoil it. He
just couldn't.

He took up the ax and put another piece of wood
on the stump he was using as a chopping block.
He hit it with such furious strength she winced.

"Are you going to ignore me?"

"I'm sure as hell going to try."

Shoshauna was a princess. She was not used
to being ignored. She was used to people doing
what she wanted them to do.

But this felt different. It felt as if she would die
if he ignored her, if they could not get back to
that place they had been at yesterday, swimming
in the magical world of a turquoise sea and

rainbow-hued fish, his hands on her back strong, cool, filled with confidence, the hands of a man who knew how to touch a woman in ways that could steal her breath, her heart, her soul.

Her sense of desperation grew. He was holding the key to something locked inside of her. How could he refuse to open that secret door? The place where she would, finally, know who she was.

"If I told my father you had done something inappropriate," she said coolly, "you'd spend the rest of your life in jail."

He gave her a look so fearless and so loaded with scorn it made her feel about six inches high. And that was when she knew he was immovable in his resolve. She knew it did not matter what she did—she could threaten him, try to manipulate him with sweetness—he was not going to do as she wanted. He had drawn his line in the sand.

And over such a ridiculously simple thing. She only wanted him to play chess with her!

Only, it wasn't really that simple, and he knew it, even if she was trying to deny it. Getting to know each other better would have complications and repercussions that could resound through both their lives.

But why worry about that today? They had so little time left. Couldn't they just go on as they had been? Couldn't they just pretend they were ordinary people in extraordinary circumstances?

But even as she thought it, she knew he would never like pretending. He was too real for that. And when she slid another look his way, she could tell by the determined set of his jaw that he intended to worry about *that* today, and she could tell something else by the set of his jaw.

She was completely powerless over him.

"I'm sorry I said that," she said, feeling utterly defeated, "about my father putting you in prison. It was a stupid thing to say, very childish."

He shrugged. "It doesn't matter." As if he *expected* her to say things like that, to act spoiled and rotten if she didn't get her own way. She had not done one thing—not one—to lead him to believe such things of her.

Unless you included saying yes to marrying a man she did not love.

That would speak volumes about her character to a man like Ronan, who wore his honor and his integrity as part of the armor around him.

"I would never do something so horrible as tell lies about you. I'm not a liar." But hadn't she lied to herself all along, about Mahail, her marriage, her life?

"I said it didn't matter," he said sharply.

"Now you really are mad at me."

He sighed heavily.

Shoshauna, looking at herself with the brutal assessment she saw in his eyes, burst into tears, ran into the house, slammed her bedroom door and cried until she had no tears left.

Shoot, Ronan thought, was she ever going to stop crying? Bastard. How hard would it have been to teach her to play chess?

It wasn't about teaching her how to play chess, he told himself sternly. It was about the fact that things were already complicated so much that she was in there crying over something as tiny as the fact he'd refused to teach her to play chess.

Though, dammit, when she had said her mother didn't want her to play chess, that it was *masculine,* something in him had just itched to give her the rudiments of the game. She had such a good mind. He bet she'd be a better-than-average player once she got the fundamentals down, probably a downright formidable one.

She didn't come out of that room for the rest of the day. When he told her he had lunch ready, she answered through the closed door, her voice muffled, that she wasn't hungry.

Now it was the same answer for supper. He should have been relieved. This was exactly what *he* needed to keep his vows. Distance. Space. Instead he felt worried about her, guilty about the pain he'd caused.

"Come on," he said, from the other side of the door, "you have to eat."

"Why? To make you feel like you've fulfilled

your obligation to look after me? Is providing a nutritious menu part of protecting me? Go away!"

He opened the door a crack. She was sitting on her bed cross-legged in those shorty-shorts that showed way too much of her gorgeous copper-toned legs. She looked up when he came in, looked swiftly back down. Her eyes were puffy from crying. Her short, boyish hair was every which way. She'd taken her bra straps off her burned shoulders, and they hung out the arms of her T-shirt.

"I told you to go away."

"You should eat something." He stepped inside the door a bit.

"You know what? I'm not a little kid. You don't have to tell me to eat."

He was already way too aware she was not a little kid. He'd seen the damned bikini once too often! He'd seen what was under the bikini, too.

He was also aware this was becoming a failure of major proportions. He was going to take her back safe from threat but damaged nonetheless:

hair chopped off, sunburned, starving, puffy-eyed from crying. Though they still had two days and a couple of hours to get through before he could cross back over that water with her, deliver her to Gray. She couldn't possibly cry that long.

His stomach knotted at the thought. Could she? He studied her to see if she was all done crying.

She'd found a magazine somewhere, and she was avoiding his eyes. The magazine looked as if it had been printed in about 1957, but she was studying it as intently as if she could read her future on the pages. Her eyes sparkled suspiciously. More tears gathering?

"Look," he said uncomfortably, shifting his weight from one foot to the other, "I'm not trying to be mean to you. I'm just telling you the way things have to be."

"Is that right?" she snapped, and threw down the magazine. She regarded him with spitting eyes, and he could see clearly it was fury in them, not tears. "As it happens, I'm sick and tired of people telling me how it's going to be. Why are

you the one who decides how it's going to be?
Because you're a man?"

She had him there.

"Because I'm the one with the job to do," he
said, but he heard the wavering of his own conviction. If ever a woman was born to be his equal
it was this one.

She hopped off the bed. Instinct told him to get
away from her. A stronger instinct told him to stay.

She stopped in front of him, regarded him with
challenge. He, foolishly, held his ground.

She reached up on tiptoe, and she took his lips
with her own.

He was enveloped in pure and sweet sensation. Her kiss was as refreshing and clean as
rainwater. Her lips told him abut the polarities
within her: innocence and passion, enthusiasm
and hesitancy, desire and doubt.

He had heard there were drugs so strong a man
could be made helpless by them after one taste.

He had never believed it until this moment. He
willed himself not to respond, but he did not

have enough will to move away from her, from the sweetness of her quest.

The hesitancy and the doubt suddenly dissolved. Her arms reached out, tangled themselves around his neck, drew him closer to her. Her scent wrapped around him, feminine, clean, intoxicating. Through the thinness of her shirt he could feel the warmth radiating off her skin. Her curves, soft, sensual, womanly, pressed into him.

Temptation was furious within him. Pure feeling tried to swamp rational thought. But the soldier in him, highly disciplined, did the clean divide between the emotion he was feeling and what he *needed* to do.

If he continued this, if he accepted the invitation of her lips, the growing urgency of her kiss, if he allowed it to go where it wanted to go, it would be like a wild horse that had broken free, allowed to run. There would be no bringing it back under rein once it had gone too far.

The soldier wanted control; the man wanted to lose control.

The soldier insisted on inserting one more fact. If this carried to its natural conclusion, Princess Shoshauna would be compromised. The wedding would be off. Her wedding. Again, she wouldn't have made a *choice,* just allowed herself to be carried along by forces she considered out of her control.

It was not what Ronan wanted for her.

He didn't want her to get married to anyone but—

But who?

Him? A soldier. A soldier who didn't believe in marriage? Who *hated* it? This must be a genetic flaw in his family, the ability to convince oneself over a very short period of time, before reality had a chance to kick in, that a marriage could work. He yanked himself away from her.

This was the difference between him and his mother: he didn't have to follow the fantasy all the way through to the end. He already knew the end of every love story.

The soldier won—fact over fiction, practical

analysis over emotion, discipline over the wayward leanings of a man's heart.

But he was aware it was a slim victory at best. And he was aware that aggravating word, *love,* had popped up again, banished from his vocabulary since around his thirteenth birthday. It was suddenly presenting itself in his life with annoying frequency.

Ronan made himself hold Shoshauna's gaze, fiery with passion, soft with surrender. He tried to force all emotion from his tone. But the magnitude of his failure to do so—the cold fury of his voice—even took him by surprise. Of course, he really wasn't angry at her, but at himself, at his own vulnerability, his own weakness, his sudden crippling wistfulness.

Hope—a sudden ridiculous wish to regain his own innocence, a desire to be able to believe in things he had long since lost faith in.

"Are you using me to buy your freedom?"

She reeled back from him. If he was not mistaken the tears were back in her eyes, all the proof he needed that insanity had grabbed him momentarily, that moment when he had contemplated her and himself and marriage in the same single thought.

The truth was much more simple. He was a soldier, rough around the edges, hardened, not suitable for the company of a princess or anyone sensitive or fragile.

But there was nothing the least bit fragile about Shoshauna when she planted both her little hands on his chest and shoved him with such amazing strength that it knocked him completely off balance. He stumbled backward, two steps, through her bedroom doorway, and she rushed forward and slammed the door behind him with the force of a hurricane.

As he contemplated the slammed door, he had the politically incorrect thought that it was a mistake that hurricanes weren't still named exclusively after women: volatile, completely unpredictable, even the strongest man could not hope to hold his balance in the fury.

"Just go straight to hell!" she yelled at him through the door. She followed that with a curse that was common among working men and soldiers, a curse so *common* her mother surely would have had heart failure hearing it come from her princess daughter's refined lips.

So he was returning Shoshauna a changed woman. No hair, sunburned, starved *and* she was going to be able to hold her own in a vocabulary contest with a construction crew.

He turned away, muttering to himself, "Well, that didn't go particularly well."

But outside, contemplating a star-studded night, black-velvet sky meeting inky-black ocean, he rethought his conclusions.

Maybe it had gone well. Shoshauna was a woman who needed to discover the depths of her own power, who needed to know how to utilize the hurricane forces within her, so she would not be so easily buffeted by the forces outside of her. In the past it seemed that every shift of wind had made her change direction.

She'd made the decision to get married because her cat died? Only his mother could come up with a fruitier reason than that!

But from the way Shoshauna had shoved him and slammed that door, she was nearly there. Could she hold on to what she was discovering about herself enough to refuse a marriage to a man she did not love? Could she understand she had within her the strength to *choose* the life she wanted for herself?

Despite the peaceful serenity of the night, contemplating such issues made his head hurt. One of the things he appreciated most about his military lifestyle was that it was a cut-and-dried world, regulated, no room for contemplation, few complexities. You did what you were trained to do, you followed orders: no question, no thought, no introspection.

He scrubbed his hand across his lips, but he had a feeling what had been left there was not going to be that easy to erase.

After a long time he looked at his watch. It was

past midnight. Just under forty-eight hours to go, and then they were leaving this island, meeting Gray.

What if her life was still in danger?

Well, if it was, if the situation was still not resolved, Gray had to have come up with a protection plan for her that did not involve Ronan.

But was he going to trust anyone else with her protection if she was still in danger? Would he have a choice? If he was ordered back to Excalibur, he was going to have to go, whether she was in danger or not.

He hoped it was a choice he was never going to have to make. Which would he obey? The call of duty or the call of his own heart?

Jake Ronan had never had to ask himself a question like that before, and he didn't like it one little bit that he had asked it now.

The fact that he had asked it meant something had shifted in him, changed. He cared about someone else as much as he cared about duty. Once you had done that, could you ever go back to the way you were before?

That's what he felt over the next twenty-four hours. That he was a man trying desperately to be what he had been before: cool, calm, professional, a man notorious for being able to control emotion in situations gone wild.

He almost succeeded, too.

It wasn't fun, and it wasn't easy, that he was managing to keep the barriers up between them. She was using the kitchen at different times than him. She refused to eat what he left out for her. He found her burnt offerings all over the kitchen, along with mashed fruit. He didn't know if she was trying to torment him by washing her underthings and stringing them on a line by the outdoor shower, but torment him it did, especially since she had managed to turn her bra from pure white to a funny shade of pink.

Of course, he could show her how to do laundry. He *wanted* to, but to what end? Nothing about her life included needing an ability to do laundry without turning her whites to pink.

And nothing about his life needed the complication of inviting her back into it.

No, this might be painful: these silences, the nose tilted upward every time she had to pass him, the hurt she was trying to hide with pride and seething silence, but in the end it was for the best. Even when he found an aloe vera plant and knew how it would soothe her sunburn, bring moisture and coolness and healing to her now badly peeling skin, he would not allow himself to make the offer.

When he saw her sitting at the dining room table by herself, moving chess pieces wistfully, he would not allow himself to give in to the sudden weakness of *wanting* to teach her how to play.

It only led to other wantings: wanting to make her laugh, wanting to see her succeed, wanting to see her tongue stuck between her teeth in concentration, wanting to touch her hair.

Wanting desperately to taste her lips again, just one more time, as if he could memorize how it felt and carry it inside him forever.

But he didn't give in to any of that. He applied every bit of discipline he had ever learned as a soldier to do what was right instead of what he wanted to do.

And he would have made it.

He would have made it right until the end, except that the wind came up.

The surf was up in the bay. And Princess Shoshauna, clad in a T-shirt to cover her burns, was running toward it, laughing with exhilaration and anticipation, the old surfboard they'd uncovered tucked under her arm.

"Hey," he yelled from the steps of the cottage, "you aren't a good enough swimmer for that water."

She glanced back. If he was not mistaken she stuck out her tongue at him. And then she ran even faster, kicking up the sand in her bare feet.

With a sigh of resignation and surrender, Ronan went after her.

CHAPTER SEVEN

SHOSHAUNA found the waves extraordinarily beautiful, rolling four feet high out in the water where they began their curl, breaking on the beach with a thunderous explosion of white foam and fury.

Her foot actually touched the hard pack of wave-pounded sand, when his hand clamped down on her shoulder with such strength it spun her.

Even though she had spent way too much time imagining his touch, it was not satisfactory in that context! She faced him, glaring. "What?" she demanded.

"You're not a strong enough swimmer for that surf."

"Well, you don't know everything! You said

the surf would never even come up in this bay and you were wrong about that!"

"I'm not wrong about this. I'm not letting you go in the water by yourself."

He had that look on his face, fierce; the warrior not to be challenged.

But Shoshauna had been counting days and hours. She knew this time of freedom was nearly over for her. Tomorrow they would be gone from here. And she knew something else. She was responsible for her own life and her own decisions.

She stood her ground, lifted her chin to him.

"I have a lifelong dream of doing this, and I'm doing it."

He looked totally unimpressed with her newfound resolve, indifferent to her discovery of her own power, immune to the sway of her life dreams. He folded his arms over his chest, set his legs, a man getting ready to throw her over his shoulder if he had to.

As delicious as it might be to be carried by him kicking and screaming up to the cottage, this was important to her, and she suddenly had to make him see that.

"It's my lifelong dream, and the waves came. Don't you think you have to regard that as a gift from the gods?"

"No."

"Ronan, all my life people have made my decisions for me. And I've let them. Starting right here and right now, I'm not letting them anymore. Not even you."

Something in him faltered. He looked at the waves and he looked at her. She could see the struggle in his face.

"Ronan, its not that I want to. I *have* to. I have to know what it feels like to ride that kind of power, to leash it. I feel if I can do that, conquer those waves, it's just the beginning for me. If I can do that, I can do anything."

And suddenly she knew she had never spoken truer words. Suddenly she realized she had made a crucial error the other night when she had thought he held the key to the secrets locked away within her.

When they had started this adventure, she remembered saying she didn't know how to find what she was looking for because she didn't know where to look.

But suddenly she knew exactly where to look.

Every answer she had ever needed was there. Right inside herself. And part of that was linked to these waves, to *knowing* what she was capable of, to tapping her sense of adventure instead of denying it. She could not ask Ronan—or anyone else—not her mother or her father or Mahail to accept responsibility for her life. She was in charge. She was taking responsibility for herself. He did not hold the key to her secrets; she did.

She knew that what she was thinking must have shown in her face, because Ronan studied her, then nodded once, and the look on his face was something she would take back with her and cherish as much, maybe more, than the satisfaction of riding the wave.

She had won Ronan's admiration—reluctant, maybe, but still there. He had looked at her, long and hard, and he had been satisfied with what he had seen.

She turned and stepped into the surf, laughed as she leaped over a tumbling wave and it crashed around her, soaking her in foam and seawater.

Then, when she was up to her knees, she placed the board carefully in front of her and tossed herself, belly down, on top of it. It was as slippery as a banister she had once greased with butter, and it scooted out from underneath her as if it was a living thing. A wave pounded over her, awesome in its absolute power, and then she got up and ran after the board.

Drenched, but deliriously happy, she caught the board, shook water from herself, tried again. And then again. It was discouraging. She couldn't even lie on it without getting dumped off. How was she ever going to surf?

Her arms and shoulders began to hurt, and it occurred to her this was going to be a lot harder than she'd been led to believe by watching surfers on TV. But in a way she was glad. She wanted it to be challenging. She wanted to test her spunk and her determination and her spirit of adventure. Life-altering moments were not meant to be easy!

Ronan came and picked her up out of the sand after she was dumped for about the hundredth time, grabbed the board that was being dragged out to sea. She grabbed it back from him.

He sighed. "Let me give you a few tips before you go back out there. The first is this: you don't *conquer* that water. You work with it, you read it, you become a part of it. Give me the board."

It was an act of trust to hand the board to him, because he could just take it and go back to the cottage, but somehow she knew he was now as committed to this as she was. There was nothing tricky about Ronan. He was refreshing in that he was such a what-you-see-is-what-you-get kind of guy.

"You're lucky," he said, "it's a longboard, not a short one, a thruster. But it's old, so it doesn't have a leash on it, which means you have to be very aware where it is at all times. This board is the hardest thing in the water, and believe me, it hurts when it clobbers you."

She nodded. He tossed the board down on the sand.

"Okay, get on it, belly down."

She recognized the gift he was giving her: his experience, and recognized her chances of doing this were better if she listened to him. And that's what he'd said. True power wasn't about conquering, it was about working *with* the elements, reading them.

And that's what Ronan was like: one of the elements, not to be conquered, not to be tamed. To be read and worked with.

When she was down on her belly, he gave her tips about positioning: how to hold her chin, where to have her weight on the board—dead center, not too far back or too far forward.

And so she learned another lesson about power: it was all about balance.

He told her how to spot a wave that was good to ride. "Nothing shaped like a C," he warned her sternly. "Look for waves shaped liked pyramids, small rollers to start with. We'll keep you here in the surf, no deeper than your hips until you get the hang of it."

He said that with absolute confidence, not a doubt in his mind that she would get the hang of it, that she would be riding waves.

"So, practice hopping up a couple of times, here on the sand. Grab the rails."

"It doesn't have rails!"

"Put your hands on the edges," he showed her, positioning her hands. She tried not to find his touch too distracting! "And then push up, bend your back and knees to start, get one leg under you, and pop up as fast as you can. If you do it slow, you'll just tip over once you're in the water."

Under his critical eye, she did it about a dozen times. If he kept this up she was going to be too tired to do it for real!

"Okay," he finally said, satisfied, peeling off his shirt and dropping it in the sand. "Let's hit the water."

They didn't go out very far, the water swirling around his hips, a little higher on her, lapping beneath her breastbone.

"This is the best place to learn, right here." He steadied the board for her while she managed to gracelessly flop on top of it.

"Don't even try to stand up the first couple of times, just ride it, get a sense for how your surfboard sleds."

"Sleds? As in snow?"

"Same word," he said, and she smiled thinking this might be as close as she got to sledding of any kind. Maybe she would have to be satisfied to look after two dreams with one activity!

"Okay, here it comes. Paddle with those arms, not too fast, just to build momentum."

Shoshauna felt the wave lift the board, paddled and then felt the most amazing thing: as if she was the masthead at the head of that wave. The board was moving with its own power now and it shot her forward with incredible and exhilarating speed. The ride lasted maybe a full two seconds, and then she was tossed onto the sand with such force it lifted her shirt and ground sand into her skin.

"Get up," he yelled, "incoming."

Too late, the next wave pounded down on top of her, ground a little more sand into her skin.

He was there in an instant hauling her to her feet.

She was laughing so hard she was choking. "My God, Ronan, is there anything more fun in the entire world than that?"

He looked at her, smiled. "Now, you're *stoked*," he said.

"Stoked?"

"Surfer word for *ready*, so excited about the waves you can barely stand it."

"That's me," she agreed, "stoked." And it was true. She felt as if she had waited her whole life to feel this: excited, alive, tingling with the awareness of possibility.

"Ready to try it standing up?"

"I'm sooo ready," she said.

"You would have made a hell of a soldier," he said with a rueful shake of his head, and she knew she had just been paid the highest of compliments.

"I want to do it myself!"

"Sweetheart, in surfing that's the only way you *can* do it."

Sweetheart. Was it the exhilaration of that offhanded endearment that filled her with a brand-new kind of power, a brand-new confidence?

She went back out, got on the board, carefully positioned herself, stomach down. She turned, watching over her shoulder for just the right wave.

She floated up and over a few rolling waves, and then she saw one coming, the third in a set of three. She scrambled, but despite her practice runs, the board was impossibly slippery beneath her feet. It popped out from under her. The wave swallowed her, curled around her, tossed her and the board effortlessly toward the shore.

She popped up, aware Ronan was right beside her, waiting, watching. But the truth was, despite a mouth full of seawater, she loved this! She loved feeling so part of the water, feeling so challenged. There was only excitement in her as she grabbed the board, swam back out and tried again. And again. And again.

Ronan watched, offered occasional advice, shouted encouragement, but he'd been right. There was only one way to do this. No one could do it for you. It was just like life. He did not even try to retrieve the board for her, did not try to help her back on it after it got away for about the hundredth time. Was he waiting for her to fail? For exhaustion and frustration to steal the determination from her heart?

But when she looked into the strong lines of his face, that was not what she saw. Not at all. She saw a man who believed she could do it and was willing to hold on to that belief, even while her own faith faded.

It was his confidence in her, the look on his face,

that made her turn the board back to shore one last time, watch the waves gathering over her shoulder. It was the look on his face that made Shoshauna feel as if she would die before she quit.

Astonishingly, everything worked. The wave came, and the crest lifted her and the board. She found her feet; they stuck to the board; she crouched at exactly the right moment.

She was riding the sea, being thrust with incredible power toward the shore.

She rode its fabulous power for less than a full second, but she rode it long enough to feel its song beneath her, to feel her oneness with that power, to taste it, to know it, to want it. Her exhaustion disappeared, replaced by exhilaration.

She was really not sure which was more exhilarating, riding the wave or having earned the look of quiet respect in Ronan's face as he came up to her, held up his hand. "Slap my hand," he told her.

She did, and felt his power as surely as she had felt that of the wave.

"That's a high five, surfer lingo for a great ride," he told her.

She achieved two more satisfactory rides before exhaustion made her quit.

He escorted her to shore. She was shivering with exhaustion and exertion and he wrapped her in the shirt he had discarded there in the sand.

"I did it!" she whispered.

"Yes, you did."

She thought of all the things she had done since they had landed on this island and felt a sigh of contentment within her. She was a different person than she had been a few short days ago, far more sure of herself, loving the glimpse she'd had of her own power, of what she was capable of doing once she had set her mind to it.

"I want to see what you can do," she said. She meant surfing, but suddenly her eyes were on his lips, and his were on hers.

"Show me," she asked him, her voice a plea. *Show me where it all can go. Show me all that a person can be.*

He hesitated, looked at her lips, then looked at the waves, the lesser of two temptations. She saw the longing in his eyes, knew he was *stoked*. She caught a glimpse of the boy he must have once been, before he had learned to ride his power, tame it, leash it.

And then he picked up the board and leaped over the crashing waves to the water beyond. He lay down on the board, paddled it out, his strength against the surging ocean nothing less than amazing. He scorned the surf that she had ridden, made his way strongly past the breakers, got up into a sitting position, straddling the board and then waited.

He rode up and over the swells, waiting, gauging the waves, patient. She saw the wave coming that she knew he would choose.

He dropped to his chest, paddled forward, a few hard strokes to get the board moving, glanced back just as the top of the wave picked up the back of his board. She saw the nose of the board lift out of the water, and then, just when she thought maybe he had missed it, in one quick snap, he was up.

He rode the board sideways, one hip toward the nose of the board, the other toward the tail, his feet apart, knees bent, arms out, his position slightly crouched. She could see him altering his position, shifting his weight with his body position to steer the board. He was actually cutting across the face of the wave, down under the curl, his grace easy, confident and breathtaking. He made it look astonishingly easy.

This was where it went, then. When a person exercised their power completely, it became a ballet, not a fight with the forces, but a beautiful, intricate dance with the elements. Ronan rode that wave with such certainty.

Shoshauna had walked all her life with men who called themselves princes, but this was the first time she had seen a man who truly owned the earth, who could be one with it, who was so comfortable with his own power and in his own skin.

There was another element to what he was doing, and she became aware of it as he outran the wave, dropped back to his stomach, moved out to catch another. He was not showing her up, not at all.

Showing *off* for her, showing her his agility and his strength and his grace in this complex dance with the sea.

He may have been mastering the sea, but he was giving in, surrendering, to the chemistry, the sizzle that had been between them from the very moment he had first touched her, dragged her to the ground out of harm's way, a mere week ago, a lifetime ago.

Ronan was doing what men had been doing for woman since time began: he was preening for her, saying, without the complication of words: *I am strong. I am fearless. I am skilled. I am the hunter, and I will hunt for you. I am the warrior, and I will protect you.*

It was a mating ritual, and she could feel her heart rising to the song he was singing to her out there on the waves.

Finally he came in, tossed the board down, then threw himself down on his stomach and lay panting in the sand beside her.

She wanted to taste his lips again, but knew she was in the danger zone. He questioned her motives, he would never allow himself to be convinced that it was about *them,* not about her looking for convenient ways to escape her destiny.

To even try to convince him might be to jeopardize the small amount of time they had left.

Tomorrow, hours away from now, they would leave here.

As if thinking the same thought, he told her his plan for the day. They would take the boat back across the water, find where the motorcycle was stashed in the shrubbery. Did she know of a fish-and-chips-style pub close to the palace? She told him that almost certainly it was Gabby's, the only British-style pub on the island that she was aware of.

"We'll meet Colonel Peterson there at three," he said.

"And then?"

"If it's safe, you'll go home. If it isn't, you'll most likely go into hiding for a little longer."

"With you?"

"No, Shoshauna," he said quietly. "Not with me."

She would have tonight, then one more ride on that motorcycle, and then, whatever happened next, *this* would be over.

Sadness threatened to overwhelm her, and she realized she did not want to ruin one moment of this time she had left contemplating what was coming. She suspected there was going to be plenty of time for sadness.

Now was the time for joy. For connection. He knew they were saying goodbye, it had relaxed his guard.

Shoshauna looked at the broadness of Ronan's shoulders as he lay in the sand beside her, how his back narrowed to the slenderness of his waist, she looked at how the wet shorts clung to the hard-muscled lines of his legs and his buttocks.

She became aware he was watching her watching him, out of the corner of his eye, letting it happen, maybe even enjoying it.

She reached out and rested her hand on the dip of his spine between his shoulders. For a minute his muscles stiffened under her touch, and she wondered if he would deprive her of this moment, get up, head to the cottage, put distance between them. She wondered if she had overplayed.

But then he relaxed, closed his eyes, let her touch him, and she thought, *See? I knew I would be a good chess player.* Still, she dared not do more than that, for fear he would move away, but she knew he was as aware as she was that their time together was very nearly over. That was the only reason he was allowing this. And so she tried to memorize the beauty of his salt- and sand-encrusted skin beneath her fingertips, the wondrous composition of his muscle and skin. She felt as if she could feel the life force flowing, vibrating, throbbing through him with its own energy, strong, pure, good.

Night began to fall, and with it the trade winds picked up and the wind chilled. She could feel the goose bumps rising on his flesh and on her own. The waves crashed on the shore, throwing fine spray droplets of water up toward them.

Still, neither of them made a move to leave this moment behind.

"Do you think we could have a bonfire tonight," she asked, "right here on the beach?"

Silence. Struggle. It seemed as if he would never answer. She was aware she was holding her breath.

"Yeah," he said, finally, gruffly. "I think we could."

She breathed again.

Ronan slid a glance at Shoshauna. She had changed into a striped shirt and some crazy pair of canvas slacks she had found in the cottage, lace-up front with frayed bottoms that made her look like an adorable stowaway on a pirate's ship.

Despite the outfit, she was changed since the surfing episode, carrying herself differently. A new confidence, a new certainty in herself. He was glad he'd let down his guard enough to be part of giving her that gift, the gift of realizing who she would be once she went back to her old world.

Surely, he thought looking at her, at the tilt of her chin, the strength in her eyes, the fluid way she moved, a woman certain of herself, she would carry that within her, she would never marry a man for convenience, or because it would please others. He remembered her hand resting on his back. Surely, in that small gesture, he had felt who she was, and who she would be.

Tonight, their last night together, he would keep his guard down, just a bit, just enough.

Enough to what? he asked himself.

To have parts of her to hold on to when he let her go, when he did not have her anymore, when he faced the fact he would probably never look at her face again.

Then he would have this night: the two of them, a bonfire, her laughter, the light flickering on her skin, the sparkle in her eyes putting the stars to shame.

In the gathering darkness they hauled firewood to the beach. As the stars came out, they roasted fish on sticks, remembered her antics in the water, laughed.

Tomorrow it would be over. For tonight he was not going to be a soldier. He was going to be a man.

And so they talked deep into the night. When it got colder, he went and got a blanket and wrapped it around her shoulders, and then when it got colder still and she held up a corner, he went and sat beneath the blanket with her, shoulder to shoulder, watching the stars, listening to the waves and her voice, stealing glimpses of her face, made even more gorgeous by the reflection of the flame that flickered across it.

At first the talk was light. He modified a few jokes and made her laugh. She told him about tormenting her nannies and schoolteachers.

But somehow as the night deepened, so did the talk. And he was hearing abut a childhood that had been privileged and pampered, but also very lonely.

She told him about the kitten she had found on a rare trip to the public market, and how she had stuck it under her dress and taken it home. She smiled as she told the story about a little kitten taking away the loneliness, how she had talked to it, slept with it, made it her best friend.

The cat had died.

"Silly, maybe to be so devastated over a cat," she said sadly, "but I can't tell you how I missed him, and how the rooms of my apartment seemed so empty once he was gone. I missed all his adorable poses, and his incredible self-centeredness."

"What was his name?"

"Don't laugh."

"Okay."

"It was Retnuh. In our language it means Beloved."

He didn't laugh. In fact, he didn't find it funny at all. He found it sad and lonely and it confirmed things about her life that she had wanted to tell him all along but that he had already guessed anyway.

"Prince Mahail's proposal came very shortly after my Beloved died. Ronan, it felt so much easier to get swept along in all the excitement than to feel what I was feeling. Bereft. Lonely. Pathetic. A woman whose deepest love had been for a cat."

But he didn't see it as pathetic. He saw it as something else: a woman with a fierce capacity to love, giving her whole heart when she decided to love, giving it her everything. Would the man who finally received that understand what a gift it was, what a treasure?

"Will you tell me something about you now?"

It was one of those trick questions women were so good at. She had shared something *deep,* meaningful. She wasn't going to be satisfied if he talked about his favorite soccer team.

"I wouldn't know where to begin," he said, hedging.

"What kind of little boy were you?" she asked him.

Ah, a logical place to begin. "A very bad one," he said.

"Bad or mischievous?"

"Bad. I was the kid putting the potatoes in the tailpipes of cars, breaking the neighbors' windows, getting expelled from school for fighting."

"But why?"

But why? The question no one had asked. "My Dad died when I was six. Not using that as an excuse, just some boys need a father's hand in their lives. My mother seemed to know she was in way over her head with me. I think wanting to get me under control was probably motivation for most of her marriages."

"*Marriages?* How many?" Shoshauna whispered, wide-eyed. This would be scandalous in her country where divorce was nearly unheard of. It had been scandalous enough in his own.

"Counting the one coming up? Seven?"

"You can't be responsible for that one!"

Still, he always felt vaguely responsible, a futile sense of not being able to protect his mother. When he was younger it was a sense of not being enough.

"What was that like for you growing up? Were any of her husbands like a father to you?" Shoshauna asked.

And for some reason he told her what he had never told anyone. About the misery and the feelings of rejection and the rebellion against each new man. He told her about how that little tiny secret spark of hope that someday he would have a father again had been steadily eroded into cynicism.

He didn't know why he told her, only that when he did, he didn't feel weaker. He felt lighter.

And more content than he had felt in many years.

"What was your mother's marriage to your father like?" she asked softly.

He was silent, remembering. Finally he sighed, and he could hear something that was wistful in him in that sigh. He had thought it was long dead, but now he found it was just sleeping.

"Like I said, I was only six when he died, so I don't know if these memories are true, or if they are as I wish it had been."

"Tell me what you think you remember."

"Happiness." He was surprised by how choked he sounded. "Laughter. I remember, one memory more vivid than any other, of my dad chasing my mom around the house, her running from him shrieking with laughter, her face alight with life and joy. And when he caught her, I remember him holding her, covering her with kisses, me trying to squeeze in between them, to be a part of it. And then he lifted me up, and they squeezed me between them so hard I almost couldn't breathe for the joy of it."

For a long time she was silent, and when she looked at him, he saw what the day had given her in her face: a new maturity, a new ability to be herself in the world.

And he heard it in her voice, in the wisdom of what she said.

She said, "Once your mother had that, what she

had with your father, I would think she could not even imagine trying to live without it. By marrying all those men, she was only trying to be alive again. Probably for you, as much as for herself. It wasn't that she wanted those men to give you something you didn't have, it was that she wanted to give you what she had been before, she saw you grieving for her as much as for him."

It was strange, but when he heard those words, he felt as if he had searched for them, been on a quest that led him exactly to this place.

A place where, finally, he could forgive his mother.

Ever since he'd left home, it was as if he had tried desperately to put a lid on the longing his earliest memories had created. He had tried to fill all the spaces within himself: with discipline, with relentless strength, with purpose, with the adrenaline rush of doing dangerous things.

But now he saw that, just like Shoshauna, he had been brought to this place to find what was really within himself.

He was a man who wanted to be loved.

And deserved to be loved.

A man who had come to know you could fill your whole world, but if it was missing the secret ingredient it was empty.

With the fire warm against their faces and the blanket wrapped around them, they slept under the winking stars and to the music of the crashing waves. He had not felt so peaceful, or so whole, for a long, long time.

But he awoke with a fighting man's instinct just before dawn.

For a moment he was disoriented, her hair, soft as eiderdown, softer than he could have ever imagined it, tickling the bottom of his chin, her head resting on his chest, her breath blowing in warm puffs against his skin.

The feeling lasted less than half a second.

He could hear the steady, but still far off, *wop-wop-wop* of a helicopter engine, beneath that the steady but still-distant whine of powerboats.

He sat up, saw the boats coming, halfway

between the island and the mainland, three of them forming a vee in the water, the helicopter zooming ahead of them to do reconnaissance.

The fire, he thought, amazed at his own stupidity. He'd been able to see the lights of the mainland from here, how could he have taken a chance by lighting that fire?

Because he'd been blinded, that's how. He'd forgotten the number-one rule of protection, no not forgotten it, been lulled into believing, that just this once it would be okay to set it aside. But he'd been wrong. He'd broken the rule he knew to be sacred in his business, and now he was about to pay the price.

He knew that emotional involvement with the principal jeopardized their well-being, their safety. And he had done it anyway, putting his needs ahead of what he knew was right.

He'd acted as if they were on a damn holiday from the moment they'd landed on this island. Instead of snorkeling and surfing, he should have spent his time creating a defensible position: hiding places, booby traps, a fall-back plan.

He felt the sting of his greatest failure, but there was no time now for self-castigation. There would probably be plenty of time for that later.

He eyed their own boat, the tide out, so far up on the sand he didn't have a chance of getting it to the water before the other boats were on them, and he didn't like the idea of being out in the open, sitting ducks. He could hear the engines of those other boats, anyway. They were far more powerful than the boat on the beach.

"Wake up," he shouted at her, leaping to his feet, his hand rough on her slender shoulder.

There was no time to appreciate her sleep-ruffed hair, her eyes fluttering open, the way a line from his own chest was imprinted on her cheek. She was blinking at him with sleepy trust that he knew himself to be completely unworthy of.

He yanked her to her feet. She caught his urgency instantly, allowed herself to be pushed at high speed toward the cottage. He stopped there only briefly to pick up the Glock, two clips of ammo, and then he led the way through the jungle, to where he had chopped down the tree earlier.

He tucked her under the waxy leaves of a gigantic elephant foot shrub. "Don't you move until I tell you you can," he said.

"You're not leaving me here!"

He instantly saw that her concern was not for herself but for him. This was the price for letting his barriers down, for not maintaining his distance and his authority. She thought listening to him was an option. She did not want to understand it was his job to put himself between her and danger.

She did not want to accept reality.

And his weakness was that for a few hours yesterday he had not accepted it either.

"Princess, do not make me say this again," he said sharply. "You do not move until you hear from me, personally, that it's okay to do so."

Three boats and a helicopter. He had to assume the worst in terms of who it was and what their intent was. That was his job, to react to worst-case scenarios. There was a good chance she might not be hearing from him, personally, ever again. He might be able to outthink those kind of numbers, but their only chance was if she cooperated, stayed out of the way.

"*My* life depends on your obedience," he told her, and saw, finally, her capitulation.

He raced back to the tree line, watched the boats coming closer and closer, cutting through the waters of the bay. His mind did the clean divide, began clicking through options of how to keep her safe with very limited resources. Not enough rounds to hold off the army that was approaching.

The boats drew closer, and suddenly he stood down. His adrenaline stopped pumping. He recognized Colonel Gray Peterson at the helm of the first boat, and he stepped from the trees.

Ronan moved slowly, feeling his sense of failure acutely. This was ending well, but not because of his competence. Because of luck.

Because of that thing she had always seemed to trust and he had scorned.

Gray came across the sand toward him.

"Where's the princess?" he asked.

"Secure."

Of course she picked that moment to break from the trees and scamper down the beach. She must have left her hiding place within seconds of Ronan securing her promise she would stay there.

"Grandpa!" She threw herself into the arms of a distinguished-looking elderly man.

Ronan contemplated her disobedience—the complete disintegration of his authority over her—with self-disgust.

Gray looked at her, his eyebrows arched upward. "Good grief, man, tell me that's not the princess."

"I'm afraid it is."

But Gray's dismay was not because she had broken cover without being given the go-ahead.

"What on earth happened to her hair?"

The truth was Ronan could only vaguely remember what she had looked like before.

"She's safe. Who cares about her hair?"

Gray's look said it all. People cared about her hair. Ronan was glad she had cut it if it made her less of a commodity.

"She is safe, isn't she?" Ronan asked. "That's why you're here? That's why you didn't wait for me to come in?"

"We made an arrest three days ago."

"Who?" He needed to know that. If it was some organized group with terror cells all over the place, she would never be safe. And what would he do then?

Peterson lowered his voice. "You gave us the lead. Princess Shoshauna's cousin, Mirassa. She was an old flame of Prince Mahail's. You've heard that expression 'Hell hath no fury like a woman scorned,' but in this case it was more like high school high jinx gone very wrong."

Ronan watched Shoshauna, felt her joy at being with her grandfather and felt satisfied that her instincts had been so correct. If she had that—her instincts—and now the ability to capture the power of the wave, she was going to be all right.

"You went deep," Gray said, "if I could have found you I would have pulled you out sooner."

Oh, yeah, he'd gone deep. Deep into territory he had no right going into, so deep he felt lost even now, as if he might never make his way out.

"But when one of the villagers saw the fire last night and reported it to her grandfather he knew right away she'd be here." Gray glanced down the beach at her, frowning. "She doesn't look like the same person, Ronan."

Ronan was silent. She was the same person. But now she had a better idea of who that was, now, he hoped she would not be afraid to let it show, to let it shine.

He was aware of Gray's sudden scrutiny, a low whistle. "Anything happen that I should know about?"

So, the changes were in him, too, in his face.

"No, sir." Nothing anybody should know about. He would have to live with the fact his mistakes could have cost her her life. Because they hadn't, no one else had to know. Ronan watched the other two boats unload. Military men, palace officials, bodyguards.

"Where's Prince Mahail?' he asked grimly.

"Why would he be here?"

"If I was going to marry her and she'd disappeared, I'd sure as hell be here." But only her grandfather had come. Not her mother. Not her father. Not her fiancé. And suddenly he understood exactly why she had loved a cat so much, the loneliness, the emptiness that had driven her to say yes instead no.

But she knew herself better now. She knew what she was capable of. As far as gifts went, he thought it was a pretty good one to give her.

Gray was looking at him strangely now, then he shook it off, saying officiously, "Look, I've got to get you out of here. Your commanding officer is breathing down my neck. Your Excalibur team is on standby waiting to be deployed. I've been told, in no uncertain terms, you'd better be back when they pull the plug. I'm going to signal the helicopter to drop their ladder."

Ronan was a soldier; he trained for the unexpected; he expected the unexpected. But somehow it caught him completely off guard that he was not going to be able to say goodbye.

The helicopter was coming in low now in response to Gray's hand signals, sand rising around it. The ladder dropped.

Don't think, Ronan told himself and grabbed the swaying rope ladder, caught it hard, pulled himself up to the first rung.

With each step up the ladder, he was aware of moving back toward his own life, away from what had happened here.

Moments later, hands were reaching out to haul him on board.

He made the mistake of looking down. Shoshauna was running with desperate speed. She looked as if she was going to attempt to grab that ladder, too, as if she was going to come with him if she could.

But the ladder was being hauled in, out of the way of her reaching hands. Had he really been holding his breath, *hoping* she would make it, hoping by some miracle she could come into his world. Was he really not ready to let go? But this was reality now, the chasms between them uncrossable, forces beyond either of their control pulling them apart.

She went very still, a small person on a beach, becoming smaller by the second. And then, standing in the center of a cyclone of dust and sand, she put her hand to her lips and sent a kiss after him. He heard the man who had hauled him in take in a swift, startled gasp at the princess's obvious and totally inappropriate show of affection for a common man, a soldier no different from him.

But he barely registered that gasp or the startled eyes of the crew turning to him.

Jake Ronan, the most pragmatic of men,

thought he felt her kiss fly across the growing chasm between him and touch his cheek, a whisper of an angel's wings across the coarseness of his whiskers, as soft as a promise.

CHAPTER EIGHT

SHOSHAUNA looked around her bedroom. It was a beautiful room: decorated in turquoises and greens and shades of cream and ivory. Like all the rooms in her palatial home, her quarters contained the finest silks, the deepest rugs, the most valuable art. But with no cat providing lively warmth, her space seemed empty and unappealing, a showroom with no soul.

She was surrounded by toys and conveniences: a wonderful sound system; a huge TV that slid behind a screen at the push of a button; a state-of-the-art laptop with Internet access; a bathroom with spa features. But today, despite all that luxury, all those things she could occupy herself with, her room felt like a prison.

She longed for the simplicity of the island, and she felt as if she had been *robbed* of her last few hours with Ronan. She had thought they would at least have one more motorcycle ride together. No, she had even been robbed of her chance to say goodbye, and to ask the question that burned in her like fire.

What next?

The answer to that question lay somewhere in the six days of freedom she had experienced. She could not go back to the way her life had been before, to the way she had been before.

Where was Ronan? She still felt shocked at the abruptness of his departure. After that final night they had shared, she had wanted to say goodbye. No, *needed* to say goodbye.

Goodbye? That isn't what she wanted to say! *Hello. I can't wait to know you better. I love the way I feel when I'm with you. You show me all that is best about myself.*

There was a knock on her door, and she leaped

off her bed and answered it, but it was one of the maids and a hairdresser.

"We've come to fix your hair," the maid said cheerfully, "before you meet with Prince Mahail. I understand he's coming this afternoon."

Shoshauna did not stand back from the door to invite them in. She said quietly but firmly, "I happen to like my hair the way it is, and if Prince Mahail would like to see me he will have to make an appointment to see if it's convenient *for me*."

And then she shut the door, her maid's mouth working soundlessly, a fish gasping out of water. For the first time since she had come back to this room, Shoshauna felt free, and she understood the truth: you could live in a castle and be a prisoner, you could live in a prison and be free. It was all what was inside of you.

A half hour later there was another knock on her door, the same maid, accompanied by a small boy, a street ragamuffin.

"He said," the maid reported snippily, "he has

something that he is only allowed to give to you. Colonel Peterson said it would be all right."

The boy shyly held out the basket he was carrying and a book.

Shoshauna took the book and smiled at him. She glanced at the book. *Chess Made Simple.* Her heart hammering, she took the basket, heard the muted little whimper even before she rolled back the square of cloth that covered it.

An orange kitten stared at her with round green eyes.

She felt tears film her eyes, knew Ronan was gone, but that he had sent her a message.

Did he know what it said to her? Not "Learn to play chess," not "Here's a kitten to take the edge off loneliness."

To her his message said he had seen the infinite potential within her.

To her his message said, "Beloved." It said that he had heard her and seen her as no one else in her life ever had.

But then she realized this gift was his farewell

gift to her. It said he would not be delivering any messages himself. Had he let his guard down so completely on that final day together because he thought he would never see her again?

Never see him *again?* The thought was a worse prison than this room—a life sentence.

She wanted to just slam her bedroom door and cry, but that was not the legacy of her week with Ronan. She had learned to be strong. She certainly had no intention of being a victim of her own life! No, she planned from this day forward to be the master of her destiny! To take charge, to go after what she wanted.

And to refuse what she didn't want.

"Tell Prince Mahail I will see him this afternoon after all," she said thoughtfully.

She realized she had to put closure on one part of her life before she began another. She did not consult her father or her mother about what she had to say to Mahail.

He was waiting for her in a private drawing room, his back to her, looking out a window.

When she entered the room, she paused for a moment and studied him. He was a slight man, but handsome and well dressed.

She saw the boy who had said to her, years ago, as he was learning to ride a pony at his family's compound, "Girls aren't allowed."

He turned and smiled in greeting, but the smile faltered when he saw her hair. She deliberately wore short sleeves so he could see the chunks of skin peeling off her arms, too.

He regained himself quickly, came to her and bowed, took both her hands.

"You are somewhat worse the wear for your adventure, I see," he said, his voice sorrowful, as if she had survived a tsunami.

"Not at all," she said, "I've never *felt* better."

Of course he didn't get that at all—that how she felt was so much more important than how she looked.

"I understand you have been unaccompanied in the presence of a man," he said. "Others might see that as a smirch on your character, but of course, I do not. I understand the man's character is unimpeachable."

She knew she should be insulted that the *man's* character was unimpeachable, but in fact it *had* been Ronan who had exercised self-control, not her. Still!

"How big of you," she said. "Of course that man saved me from a situation largely of your making, but why think of that?"

"My making?" the prince stammered.

"You were cruel and thoughtless to Mirassa. She didn't deserve that, and she retaliated. I'm not excusing what she did, but I am saying I understand it."

The prince was beginning to look annoyed, not used to anyone speaking their mind around him, especially a woman. What kind of prison would that be? Not being able to be honest with the man you shared the most intimate things in the world with?

"And that man, whom *others* might see as

having put a smirch on my character, was absolutely devoted to protecting me. He was willing to put my well-being ahead of his own." *To refuse everything I offered him, if he felt it wasn't in my best interests.*

"How noble," the prince said, but he was watching her cautiously. She wasn't supposed to speak her mind, after all, just toss her hair and blink prettily.

"Yes," she agreed, "noble." Ronan, her prince, so much more so than this man who stood in front of her in his silk and jewels, the aroma of his expensive cologne filling the room.

What would he say if she said she would rather smell Ronan's sweat? She smiled at the thought, and Mahail mistook the smile for a change in mood, for coy invitation.

"Are you well enough, then, to reschedule the day of our marriage?" he asked formally.

So, despite the hair, the skin, her new outspokenness, he was not going to call it off, and suddenly she was glad, because that made it her choice, rather than his—that made it her power that had to be utilized.

She needed to *choose*.

"I've decided not to marry," she said firmly, with no fear, no doubt, no hesitation. A bird within her took wing.

"Excuse me?" Prince Mahail was genuinely astonished.

"I don't want to get married. I have so many things I want to achieve first. When I marry I want it to be for love, not for convenience. I'm sorry."

He glared at her, put out. "Have you consulted your father about this?"

Of all the maddening things he could have said, that about topped her list!

"It's my choice," she said dangerously, "not his."

Prince Mahail looked at her, confused, irritated, annoyed. "Perhaps it is for the best," he decided. "I think I might like your cousin, Mirassa, better than you after all."

"You would," Shoshauna muttered as he marched from the room.

And yet the next day, when she met with her father, she felt terrible trepidation, aware her legs were shaking under her long skirt.

Meetings with him always had a stilted quality, formal, as if his children were more his subjects than his blood.

"I understand," he said, without preamble, "that you have told Prince Mahail there will be no wedding."

"Yes, Father."

"Without consulting me?" he asked with a raised eyebrow.

Shoshauna took a deep breath and told him who she was. She did not tell him she was the girl he wanted her to be, meek, docile, pliable, but she told him of longing for education and adventure…and love.

"And so you see," she finished bravely, "I cannot marry Mahail. I am prepared to go to the dungeon first."

Her father's lips twitched, and then he laughed. "Come here," he said.

As she stepped toward him, he stood up and embraced her. "I want for you what every father wants for his daughter—your happiness. A father thinks he knows best, but you have always been a strong-spirited girl, able, I think, to find your own way. Do you want to go to school?"

"Yes, Father!"

"Then it will be arranged, with my blessing."

As she turned to go, he called her back.

"Daughter," he said, laughing, "we don't have a dungeon. If we did I suspect your poor mother would have locked you away in it a long time ago. I will explain this, er, latest development to her."

"Thank you."

Funny, she thought walking away, her whole life she had sought her father's love and approval. And she had gotten it, finally, not when she had tried to please him, but when she had been brave enough to please herself, brave enough to be herself.

This was news she had to share with Ronan. She asked Colonel Peterson where he was.

He looked at her carefully. "He's been

deployed," he said, "even if I knew where he was, I wouldn't be able to tell you."

And then she realized that was the truth Ronan had tried to tell her about his life.

And she recognized another truth: if you were going to be with a man like that, you had to have a life—satisfying and fulfilling—completely separate from his. If Ronan was going to be a part of her life, she had to come to him absolutely whole, certainly able to function when his work called him to be away.

She renewed her application for school and was accepted. In two months she would be living one more dream. She would be going to study in Great Britain.

And until then?

She was going to learn to surf! There was no room in a world like Ronan's for a woman who was needy or clingy. She needed to go to him a woman confident in her ability to make her own life.

And then she would be a woman who could make a life with him.

* * *

An alarm was going off, and men were pouring through the doors of an abandoned warehouse, men in black, their faces covered, machine guns at the ready. Ronan was with Shoshauna, his body between her and the onslaught, but he felt things no soldier ever wanted to feel—outnumbered, hopeless, helpless. He couldn't protect her. He was only one man...

Ronan came awake, drenched in sweat, grateful it wasn't real, perturbed that after six months he was still having that dream, was unable to shake his sense of failure.

Slowly he became aware that the alarm from his dream was really his phone ringing. He'd picked up the phone, along with a whole pile of other things he needed, when he'd moved off base a few months ago. Next time he bought a phone, he'd know to test the damned ringer first. This one announced callers with the urgency of an alarm system announcing a break-in at the Louvre.

He got up on one elbow and looked at the caller ID window.

"Hi, Mom," he said.

"Are you sleeping? It's the middle of the day."

"We're just back from a deployment. I'm a little turned around."

Six months ago he wouldn't have imagined voluntarily giving his mother that information, but then, six months ago she would have been asking all kinds of questions about what he'd been up to, trying to get him to quit his job, do something safer.

Interestingly, Ronan found he wasn't enjoying the emergency call-outs the way he once had. He recognized that adrenaline had become his fix, his drug, it had filled something in him.

It didn't work anymore. Not since B'Ranasha. He'd felt something else then, softer, kinder, ultimately more real.

Adrenaline had been a substitute, a temporary solution to a permanent problem. Loneliness. Yearning.

He'd been asked if he would consider taking an instructor's position with Excalibur. Maybe he was just getting older, but the idea appealed.

Now his mother didn't even ask a single detail about the deployment, which was good. Even though she now had her own life and it had made her so much more accepting of his, Ronan thought it might set their growing trust in each other back a bit if he told her he'd just been behind the lines in a country where a military coup was in full swing rescuing the deposed prime minister.

Or, he thought, listening to the happiness in her voice, maybe not.

The big news that she had been trying to reach him about when he'd taken the wedding security position on B'Ranasha, amazingly, had nothing to do with another wedding, or at least not for her. No, she'd had an idea.

She'd wanted to know if he would invest in her new company.

But of course, that wasn't really what she had

been asking. Sometime, probably in that week with Shoshauna, Ronan had developed the sensitivity to know this.

She was *really* asking for an investment in her. She was asking him, fearfully, painfully, *courageously,* to believe in her. One last time, despite it all, *please.*

And isn't that what love did? Believed? Held the faith even in the face of overwhelming evidence that to believe was naive?

The truth was he had all kinds of money. He'd had a regular paycheck since leaving high school. Renting this apartment was really the first time he'd spent any significant amount of it. His lifestyle had left him with little time and less inclination to spend his money.

Why not gamble it? His mother wanted to start a wedding-planning service and a specialized bridal boutique. Who, after all, was more of an expert on weddings than his mother? There was no *sideways* feeling in his stomach—not that he was at all certain it worked anymore—so he'd invested.

When she'd told him she'd decided on a name for their new company, he'd expected the worst.

"'Princess,'" she said, "the *princess* part in teeny letters. That's important. And then in big letters 'Bliss.'"

Into his telling silence she had said, "You hate it."

That was putting it mildly. "I guess I just don't understand it."

"No, you wouldn't, but Ronan, trust me, every woman dreams of being a princess, if only for a day. Especially on *that* day."

And then Ronan had been pleasantly surprised and then downright astounded at his mother's overwhelming success. Within a few months of opening, Princess Bliss had been named by *Aussie Business* as one of the top-ten new businesses in the country. His mother had been approached about franchising. She was arranging weddings around the globe.

"Kay Harden just called," his mother told him breathlessly. "She and Henry Hopkins are getting married again."

"Uh-huh," Ronan said.

"Do you even know who they are, Jacob?"

"No, ma'am."

"Don't call me that! Jacob, you're hopeless. Movie stars. They're both movie stars."

He didn't care about that, he'd protected enough important people to know the truth. One important person in particular had let him know the truth.

All people, inside, were the very same.

Even soldiers.

"We're going to have a million-dollar year!" his mother said.

Life was full of cruel ironies: Jake Ronan the man who hated weddings more than any other was going to get rich from them. He'd told his mother he would be happy just to have his initial investment back, but she was having none of it. He was a full, if silent, partner in Princess Bliss, if he liked it or not. And when he saw how happy his mother was, for the first time in his memory since his father had died, he liked it just fine.

"Mom," he said. "I'm proud of you. I really am. Please, don't cry."

But she cried, and talked about her business, and he just listened, glancing around his small apartment while she talked. This was another change he'd made since coming home from B'Ranasha.

After a month back at work he had decided to give up barrack life and get his own place. The brotherhood of his comrades was no longer as comfortable as it once had been. After he'd gotten back from B'Ranasha he had felt an overwhelming desire to be alone, to create his own space, a life separate from his career.

If the apartment was any indication, he hadn't really succeeded. Try as he might to make it homey, it just never was.

Try as he might to never think about *her* or that week on the island, he never quite could. He was changed. He was lonely. He hurt.

The apartment was just an indication of something else, wanting *more,* wanting to have more to life than his work.

And all that money piling up in his bank account, thanks to his partnership in Bliss, was an indication that something *more* wasn't about money, either.

He'd contacted Gray Peterson once, a couple of days after leaving B'Ranasha. He'd been in a country so small it didn't appear on the map, in the middle of a civil war. Trying to sound casual, which was ridiculous given the lengths he'd gone to, to get his hands on a phone, and hard to do with gunfire exploding in the background, he'd asked if she was all right.

And found out the only thing he needed to know: the marriage of Prince Mahail and Princess Shoshauna had been called off. Ronan had wanted to press for details, called off for what reason, by *whom,* but he'd already known that the phone call was inappropriate, that a soldier asking after a princess was not acceptable in any world that he moved in.

Ronan heard a knock on his door, got up and

answered it. "Mom, gotta go. Someone's at the door."

Was it Halloween? A child dressed as a motorcycle rider stood on his outside step, all black leather, a helmet, sunglasses.

And then the sunglasses came off, and he recognized eyes as turquoise as the sunlit bay of his boyhood. His mouth fell open.

And then she undid the motorcycle helmet strap, and struggled to get the snug-fitting helmet from her head.

He had to stuff his hands in his pockets to keep from helping her. Finally she had it off.

He studied her hair. Possibly, her hair looked even worse than it had on the island, grown out considerably but flattened by the helmet.

"What are you doing here?" he asked gruffly, as if his heart was not nearly pounding out of his chest, as if he did not want to lift her into his arms and swing her around until she was shrieking with laughter. As if he had not known, the moment he had recognized her, that she was the something *more* that he yearned for, that filled him with restless energy and a sense of hollow emptiness that nothing seemed to fill.

This was his greatest fear: that with every moment he'd dedicated to helping her find her own power, he had lost some of his own.

"What am I doing here?" she said, with a dangerous flick of her hair. "Try this—'Shoshauna, what a delightful surprise. I'm so glad to see you.'"

He saw instantly she had come into her own in ways he could not even imagine. She exuded the confidence of a woman sure of herself, sure of her intelligence, her attractiveness, her power.

"I'm going to university here now."

That explained it. Those smart-alec university guys were probably all over her. He tried not to let the flicker of pure jealousy he felt show. In fact, he deliberately kept his voice remote. "Oh? Good for you."

She glared at him, looked as if she wanted to stamp her foot or slap him. But then her eyes, smoky with heat, rested on his lips, and he knew she didn't want to stamp her foot or slap him.

"I didn't get married," she announced in a soft, husky purr.

"Yeah, I heard." No sense telling her he had celebrated as best he could, with a warm soda in one hand and his rifle in the other, watching the sand blow over a hostile land, *wishing* he had someone, something more to go home to. Feeling guilty for being distracted, wondering if he was just like his mother. Did all relationships equal a surrender of power? Wasn't that his fear of love?

"But I have dated all kinds of boys."

"Really." It was a statement, not a question. He tried not to feel irritated, his sense of having given her way too much power over him confirmed! Seeing her after all this time, all he wanted to do was taste her lips, and he had to hear she was dating guys? *Boys.* Not men. Why did he feel faintly relieved by that distinction?

"I thought I should. You know, go out with a few of them."

"And you stopped by to tell me that?" He folded his arms more firmly over his chest, but something twinkled in her eyes, and he had a feeling his defensive posture was not fooling her one little bit. She knew she had stormed his bastions, taken down his defenses long ago.

"Mmm-hmm. And to tell you that they were all very boring."

"Sorry."

"And childish."

"Males are slow-maturing creatures," he said. Had she kissed any of them, those boys she had dated? Of course she had. That was the way things worked these days. He remembered all too well the sweetness of her kiss, felt something both possessive and protective when he thought of another man—especially a childish one—tasting her.

"I didn't kiss anyone, though," she said, and the twinkle in her eyes deepened. Why was it she seemed to find him so transparent? She had always insisted on seeing who he really was, not what he wanted her to see.

He wanted to tell her he didn't care, but he had the feeling she'd see right through that, too, so he kept his mouth shut.

"I learned to surf last summer. And I can ride a motorcycle now. By myself."

"So I can see."

"Ronan," she said softly, "are you happy to see me?"

He closed his eyes, marshaled himself, opened them again. "Why are you here, Shoshauna?"

Not princess, a lapse in protocol that she noticed, too. She beamed at him.

"I want to play you a game of chess."

He didn't move from the doorway. A game of chess. He tried not to look at her lips. A game of chess was about the furthest thing from his poor, beleaguered male mind. "Why?" he croaked.

"If I win," she said softly, "you have to take me on a date."

He could have gotten her killed back there on that island. She apparently didn't know or didn't care, but he was not sure he'd ever be able to forgive himself or trust himself either.

"I can't take you on a date," he said.

"Why not? You aren't in charge of protecting me now."

If he was, she sure as hell wouldn't be riding a motorcycle around by herself. But he only said, "Good thing, since I did such a crack-up job of it the first time."

"What does that mean?"

"Don't you ever think what could have happened if those boats that arrived that day hadn't been the colonel and your grandfather? Don't you ever think of what might have happened if it hadn't been your cousin, if it had been a well-organized terror cell instead?"

There it was out, and he was glad it was out. He felt as if he had been waiting months to make this confession. Why was it always so damned easy to show her who he really was? Flawed, vulnerable, an ordinary man under his warrior armor.

"No," she said, regarding him thoughtfully, *seeing* him, "I don't. Do you?"

"I think of the possibilities all the time. I didn't do my job, Shoshauna, I just got lucky."

"The boys at school use that term sometimes," she said, her voice sultry.

"Would you be serious? I'm trying to tell you something. I can't be trusted with you. I've never been able to protect the people I love the most." The look wouldn't leave her face, as if she thought he was adorable, and so he rushed on, needing to convince her, very sorry the word *love* had slipped out, somehow. "I have this thing, this *sideways* feeling, that tells me what to do, an instinct, that warns of danger."

"What's it doing right now?" she asked.

"That's just it. It doesn't work around you!"

She touched his arm, looked up at him, her eyes so full of acceptance of him that something in him stilled. Completely.

"You know why it doesn't work around me, Ronan? Because nothing is wrong. Nothing was wrong on the island. You were exactly where you needed to be, doing exactly what you needed to do. And so was I."

"I forgot what I was there to do and, Shoshauna, that bugs the hell out of me. I didn't do a good job of protecting you. I didn't do my job, period."

"I seem to still be here, alive and kicking."

"Not because of anything I did," he said stubbornly.

She regarded him with infinite patience. "Ronan, there are some things that are bigger than even you. Some things you just have to surrender to."

"That's the part you don't get! *Surrender* is not in any soldier's vocabulary!"

She sighed as if he was being impossible and childish just like those boys she had dated. "Thank you for the kitten, by the way. I was able to bring him with me. He's a monster. I called him Hope."

He wasn't really done discussing his failures with her, but he said reluctantly, "That sounds like a girl's name." The name said it all, named the thing within him that he had not been able to outrun, kill, alter.

He *hoped.* He hoped for the life he saw promised in her eyes: a life of connection, companionship, laughter, *love.*

"You know what I think, Ronan?"

"You're going to tell me if I want to know or not," he said.

"Just like I want someone to see me for who I am, someone I don't have to put on the princess costume for, you want someone to see you without your armor. You want someone to know there is a place where you are not all strength and sternness. You want someone to see you are not all warrior."

"No, I don't!"

"Now," she said, casually, as if she had not ripped off his mask and left him feeling trembling and vulnerable and on the verge of surrendering to the mightiest thing of all, "let's play chess. I told you the terms—if I win you have to take me on a date."

"And if I win?" he asked.

She smiled at him, and he saw just how completely she had come into herself, how confident she was.

"Ronan," she said softly, her smile melting him, "why on earth would you want to win?"

CHAPTER NINE

"I CAN'T believe you'd ever accept anything but my very best effort," he said, though the truth was he already knew he was lost.

She contemplated him. "That's true. So if you win?"

"I haven't even agreed to play yet!"

"Well, we've stood at this point before, haven't we, Ronan? Where you have to decide whether or not to let me in."

They had stood at this point before. On the island he'd refused to play chess with her, and he'd made her cry. But then he had only been doing his job, and in the end that barrier had not been enough to keep him from caring about her.

Without that barrier where would it go?

A single word entered his mind. And oddly enough, it was not surrender. *Bliss.*

He stood back from his door, an admission in his heart. He was powerless against her; he had been from the very beginning. Princess Shoshauna of B'Ranasha walked into his humble apartment, took off the black jacket and tossed it on his couch as if she belonged here.

The form-fitting white silk shirt and black leather pants were at least as sexy as that bikini she had nearly driven him crazy in, and his feeling of powerlessness increased.

She looked around his place with interest. He shoved a pair of socks under the couch with his foot. She looked at him.

"I want to live in a cute little place just like this, one day."

His mother had claimed that every girl wanted to be a princess, but somehow, someway he had lucked into something very different. A girl who had already been a princess and who wanted to be ordinary.

He got his chess set out of a cabinet, set it up at the small kitchen table.

"Why didn't you call me?" she asked, sitting down, taking a black and a white chess piece and holding them out to him, closed fist.

He chose. Black, then. Let her lead the way.

He snorted. "Call you? You're a princess. You're not exactly listed in the local directory."

"You knew how to get ahold of me, though, if you'd wanted to."

"Yes."

"So you didn't want to?"

He was silent, contemplating her first move, her opening gambit. He made a defensive move.

"I couldn't. I still dream about what could have happened on that island. I failed you. There I was snorkeling and surfing, when really I should have been setting up defenses."

"I'd been protected all my life. You didn't fail me. You gave me what I needed far more than safety. A wake-up call. A call to live. To be myself. You gave me a gift, Ronan. Even when you didn't call it that, it was a gift."

He waited.

"I needed to choose and I have. I've chosen."

"To play chess with a soldier?"

"No, Ronan," she said gently. "It was never about the chess."

"So I see." He was surrendering to her, just as he had on the island, even though he didn't want to, even though he knew better. *Bliss*. It unfolded in him like a sail that had finally caught the wind, it filled him, it carried him forward into a brand-new land.

She beat him soundly at chess, though he might have been slightly distracted by the scent of her, by the pure heaven of having her in the same room again, by the sound of her voice, the light in her eyes, the way she ran her hand through the disaster that was her hair.

"Do you know why I dated those other boys?" she asked.

He shook his head.

"So that you wouldn't have one single excuse to say no to me. So that you couldn't say, 'You only think you love me. You don't know anyone else.'"

"Love?" he said.

She sighed. "Ronan, I made it perfectly clear it wasn't about the chess game."

That was true, she had.

"So," he said, "what do you want to do for that date?"

What would a princess want to do? The opera? Live theater? Was he going to have to get a new wardrobe?

"Oh," she said, " I want to go to a pub for fish and chips and then to a movie after. Just like an ordinary girl."

His mother had been so wrong. Not every girl wanted to be a princess, not at all. Still, when he looked at her and smiled, he knew there was no hope she would ever be an ordinary girl, either.

And suddenly it came to him, a truth that was at the very core of humanity. A truth that was humbling and reassuring at the very same time.

Love was more powerful than he was.

He got up from his chair, came around to hers and tugged her out of it. Shoshauna came into his arms as if she was coming home.

"I guess," he whispered against her hair, "it's time for you to start calling me Jake."

He picked her up for their first official date three nights later. He felt like a teenager getting ready. He wore jeans and a T-shirt, trying for just the right note of casual.

As he approached her address, he was aware that for a man who had done the most danger-ous things in the world with absolute icy calm, his heart was beating faster, and his palms were sweat-slicked.

She lived on campus in what looked to be a very ordinary house until he went to the front door, rang the bell and was let in.

There were girls everywhere, short girls, tall girls, skinny girls, heavy girls. There were girls dressed to go to nightclubs and girls in their pajamas. There were girls with their hair in rollers and girls hidden behind frightening facial masks of green creams and white creams. And it seemed when he stood in that front foyer, every single one of them stopped and looked at him. Really looked.

"Sexy beast," one of them called out. "Who are you here for?"

The last time he had blushed was when Shoshauna had kissed him on the cheek and called him Charming in that little market in B'Ranasha. She was determined to put him in predicaments that stretched him! At least now he knew a little blush wouldn't kill him.

"I'm here for Shoshauna." There were groans and calls of "lucky girl," and he found himself blushing harder.

But when he saw her, coming down the steps, two at a time, flying toward him, all thought of himself, of his wild discomfort at finding himself, a man so used to a man's world, so surrounded by women, was gone.

There was a look on her face when she saw him that he knew he would never forget, not if he lived to be 102.

It was unguarded and filled with tenderness.

A memory niggled at him, of a moment a long, long time ago. His father coming up the steps from work, in combat uniform, his mother running to meet him, a look just like the one on Shoshauna's face now in her eyes. And he remembered how his father had looked at her. Despite the uniform, in that moment his father had not been a warrior. No, just a man, filled with wonder, gentled by love, amazed.

In the next few weeks, even though Ronan had to run the gauntlet of her housemates every time he saw her, he spent every moment he could with her. Every second they could wangle away from hectic schedules, they were together. Simple moments—a walk, holding hands, eating pizza, playing darts at the pub—simple moments became infused with a light from heaven.

Ronan was aware that, left to his own devices, he would have performed his duties perfectly on

B'Ranasha. He would have been a perfect professional, he would never have allowed himself to become personally involved with the principal.

And he would have missed this: the tenderness, the sweetness of falling head over heels in love. But somehow, some way, a kind universe had taken pity on him, given him what he needed the most, even though he had been completely unaware of that need. Even though he had strenuously denied that need and tried to fight against it.

Falling in love with Shoshauna was like waking from a deep hypnotic state. When he woke in the morning, his first thought was of her. He felt as if he was living to make her laugh, to feel the touch of her hand, to become aware of her eyes resting on his face, something in them so unguarded and so breathtakingly, exquisitely beautiful.

For some reason he, a rough soldier, had come to be loved by a woman like this one. He planned to be worthy of it.

* * *

Shoshauna looked around, let the trade winds lift her hair. There was a flower-laced pagoda set up on the beach, the royal palace of B'Ranasha white and beautiful in the background. They had tried to keep things small, but even so the hundred chairs facing the wedding pagoda were filled. The music of a single flute intertwined with the music of the waves that lapped gently on the sand.

Jake's mother, Bev, had managed to get over her disappointment that, despite the fact it was a royal wedding, her first, they wanted nothing elaborate. Now Shoshauna saw why her mother-in-law's business was so successful: she had read their hearts and given them exactly what they wanted—simplicity—the beauty provided by the ocean, the white-capped waves in the blue bay the perfect backdrop to the day.

Shoshauna wore a simple white sheath, her feet were bare, she had a single flower in her hair.

She watched from the tree line as Jake made his way across the sand and felt the tears rise in her eyes. *Beloved.*

He was flanked by Gray Peterson, just as he had been the first time she had seen him, but this time Jake looked calm and relaxed, a man at ease despite the formality of the black suit he was wearing, the people watching him, the fact it was his wedding day.

It had been almost a year since she had first laid eyes on him, six months since she had won her first date with him in that chess match.

Since then there had been so much laughter as they discovered a brand-new world together—a world seen through the viewfinder of love.

They had ridden motorcycles, gone to movies, walked hand in hand down rain-filled streets, played chess and done nothing at all. Everything was equally as astounding when she did it with him.

He was so full of surprises. Who would have ever guessed he had such a romantic nature hidden under that stern exterior? The kitten as a gift should have been her first clue! He was constantly surprising her with heartfelt or funny little gifts: a tiara he'd gotten at a toy store; a laser pointer that drove the kitten, Hope, to distraction; a book of poems; a pink bikini that she would use now, for the first time, on her honeymoon.

And the stern exterior was just that. An exterior. She'd always thought he was good-looking, but now the hard lines on his face were relaxed around her, and the stern mask was gone from his eyes. The remoteness was gone from him and so was his need to exercise absolute control over everything. Jake Ronan seemed to have enjoyed every second of letting go of control, seeing where life—and love—would take them, if they gave it a chance.

It had taken them to this day and this moment. He stood at the pagoda, his eyes searched the tree line until they found her.

And he smiled.

In his smile she saw such welcome and such wonder—and such sensual promise—that her own heart beat faster.

Of course, there was one thing they had not done, one area where he had maintained every ounce of his formidable discipline. Jake Ronan had proven to be very old-fashioned when it came to the question of her virtue.

Oh, he had kissed her until she had nearly died from wanting him, he had touched her in ways that had threatened to set her heart on fire, but always at the last moment he had pulled away. He had told her his honor was on the line, and she had learned you did not question a warrior's honor!

But tonight she would lie in his arms, and they would discover the breathtaking heights of intimacy. After the reception, they would take her grandfather's boat, and they would go to *their* island, Naidina Karobin, *my heart is home*. The island would be once again inhabited only by them.

Last night, even though he wasn't supposed to see her until today, Jake had managed to charm his way past all her girlfriends and her cousins and aunts.

"I brought you a wedding present."

"You're not supposed to be here," she told him,

but not with a great deal of conviction. She loved seeing him.

"I know. I couldn't stay away. Knowing you were here, just a few minutes away from me, I couldn't not be with you. Shoshauna, that's what you do to me. Here I am, just about the most disciplined guy in the world, and I'm helpless around you. Worse," he moved closer to her, touched her cheek with the familiar hardness of his hands, "I like being helpless. You make me want to be with you all the time. You make everything that is not you seem dull and boring and like a total waste of time.

"You make me feel as if all those defenses I had, had kept me prisoner in a world where I was very strong but very, very alone. You rescued me."

Her eyes filled with tears. "Ronan, you could not have given me a more beautiful gift than those words."

He smiled, a little bit sheepishly. "There's still enough soldier in me that I don't see words as any kind of gift." He opened the door and brought in what he had left in the hallway.

She burst out laughing. That's what he did to her, and for her—took her from tears to laughter and back again in the blink of an eye.

A brand-new surfboard, and she had been delighted, but at the same time she rather hoped, much as she was *stoked* about surfing, that the waves would never come up. She rather hoped they would never get out of bed! Not for the whole two weeks. That she could touch him until she had her fill of the feel of his skin under her fingertips, until she had her fill of the taste of his lips, and she already knew she was never going to get her fill of that!

Shoshauna was still blushing from the audacity of her own thoughts when her mother and her father came up beside her, not a king and a queen today but proud parents. Each of them kissed her on the cheek and then took their seats.

Her father in particular was very taken with Jake. Her mother had been more slow to come around, but no one who truly got to know Jake could do anything but love him.

Her mother had also been appalled by the simplicity of the wedding plans, but she and Bev had managed to console each other and had become quite good friends as they planned the wedding of their children.

Her grandfather came to her side, linked his arm through hers, smiled at her, though his eyes were wet with tears of joy.

And then Shoshauna was moving across the sand toward her beloved, toward Jake Ronan, and she could see the whole future in his eyes. Her grandfather let her go, and she walked the last few steps to him on her own, a woman who had chosen exactly the life she wanted for herself.

Jake watched Shoshauna move toward him across the fineness of the pure white sand.

She had chosen the simplest of dresses, her feet were bare, but when you were as beautiful as she was, even his mother had agreed that simplicity was the best way to let her true beauty shine through.

His mother and his wife-to-be, here together.

And in him the most wonderful surrender. He would protect them with his life, if he ever had to, and they both knew that.

Someday he would have children with Shoshauna, and he could feel the fierce protectiveness within himself extend to them, but something new was there, too.

A trust, that he would do whatever he could do, but when his strength ran dry, then there would be *something* else there to step in, *something* that seemed to have a better plan for him than anything he could have ever planned for himself, if the woman walking over the sand toward him was any indication.

He knew that *something* went by a great many names. Some called it the Universe, the life force, God.

He had come to call it Love, and to recognize it had been running the show long before he'd come along, and would be running it long after.

There came a point when a man had to realize

that there were things he did not control, and that he would only exhaust himself, drain away his strength and his soul, if he continued to think the whole world would fall apart if he was not running it.

Ronan had come to believe that he could trust the protection and care of a force larger than himself.

It was the same force that brought a certain man and a certain woman together, against impossible odds, across cultural and social differences, the force that made one heart recognize another.

And it was that force that would protect them and see their children into the world.

Once upon a time Jake Ronan had thought if he ever had to stand where he was standing today, he would probably faint.

And yet the truth was, he had never felt so calm, so strong, so *right*. And the strangest thing of all was that, even as Ronan admitted he was powerless in the face of this thing called love, with each day of his surrender he felt more powerful, more alive and more relaxed, more grateful, more everything.

This was the something *more* he had longed for all his life: to be a part of the magnificent mystery that flowed around him and in him as surely as it flowed through the waves on the sea. He longed to ride that incredible energy with the ease and joy with which he could ride the most powerful of waves. Not to conquer but to feel connected.

He watched Shoshauna move toward him, and he almost laughed out loud.

For one thing he had come to know that this thing he chose to call Love had the most delicious sense of humor.

And for the longest time he had thought it was his job to rescue the princess.

But now he saw that wasn't it at all.

That she had come to rescue him. And that allowing himself to be rescued had not made him a weaker man but a better one.

She reached him, looked him in the face, his equal, the woman who would be the mother of his children, his companion, his friend, his lover through all the days of his life.

"Beloved," she said, her voice hushed with reverence of what they stood in the presence of, that Force greater than all things. "Retnuh."

And he said to her, his eyes never leaving her face, in her own language, a greeting and a vow, "My heart is home."